TRAP PRINCESS

By: Author Barbie Amor
Formally known as Barbie Scott

This is a work of fiction. All of the characters, organizations, and events portrayed in this novel are either products of the author's imagination or are used fictitiously. Any resemblance to actual persons, living or dead is purely coincidental.

"Life After Love"
Standing in the light of your halo
I got my angel now...

PROLOGUE

"**D**uring the surgery, the bone was cut to create two separate bone segments. This surgical procedure is called an osteotomy. We also performed an additional soft-tissue procedure to prepare the muscles and nerves for lengthening. Which is an orthopedic lengthening device to the bone. This entire procedure is called Limb Replantation. This is one of the most complex surgeries ever performed. This procedure allows patients to have severed limbs reattached after experiencing traumatic injuries."

"So, Doctor Stine, what happens after the replantation?"

"After replantation, the bones are allowed to rest for five to seven days to begin the healing process. This period of time is called the latency period. After the latency period, the patient will adjust the orthopedic device daily so that it slowly pulls apart the two bone segments. The gradual process of slowly separating the two bone segments is called distraction. The distraction phase is followed by the consolidation phase, where the regenerate bone slowly hardens. The new bone will not be healed until the regenerate bone has hardened and calcified. After the regenerate bone has fully consolidated, the orthopedic lengthening device can be removed."

"So how long after will the patient be able to walk again?"

"It's really up to the patient. However, this gentleman is a warrior. I'd say give or take about ten years. This type of surgery is more common for upper extremities like arms, hands, and fingers. Some surgeons can't pull this off. But with the help of this team, we made it possible. Let's give a round of applause to Doctor Wang, who is a specialist in difficult tissue and wound repair cases." Everyone

began to clap. "Doctor Gregory, our organ cardiovascular surgeon."
Again, everyone cheered. "The second stage of operation was much
more challenging, but thanks to Doctor Acosta, he made it happen."
Everyone began to clap a third time. Anyone who didn't know any
better would think there was a football game taking place behind the
walls of Doctor Stine's office. However, the Doctor that the world considered an Einstein, was celebrating the reincarnation of a man who
would regain life in a world that was once ripped away.

"Doctor Stine, isn't this procedure illegal?"

Doctor Stine looked over to the timid doctor who had not
spoken one word during the meeting. He watched her closely over the
rim of his small-framed glasses attentively.

"We'll deal with that when the time comes."

17 YEARS LATER...

"**C**ome on, Abdullah. You got this. Now pick up that bell for the deadlifts. Attaboy. Bend more in the knees, chest up."

"Grrr, rrrrrr, rrrrr."

"Time. Durable rope. Brace your legs, tighten your core."

Dr. Stine stepped back and watched as a muscular Abdullah pulled the powerful rope that was attached to a sled with 260 pounds of weights. The small smirk crept up on his face because he was proud of his accomplishment. It had been a long time coming, and after seventeen long years, "the project", as he referred, had blossomed into something electrifying. Not only had Abdullah been restored, he transitioned into nearly a bodybuilder. He was huge, muscular and still possessed those same killer instincts. After writing several novels, he was currently ready to take the world by a storm when he released the biggest motion picture of all time: Halo. A masterpiece in the making.

Right now, the doctor didn't have an ending for a sequel, but something told him that in due time, he'd have an ending that would earn him a few awards and make him a very rich man. Doctor David Stine was ready to retire, and now that Abdullah was fully recovered, the time had come for him to focus on himself.

"Good Job." Doctor Stine patted Abdullah on the back, and Abdullah slightly moved.

Doctor Stine stepped back nervously because he didn't mean to offend him. Abdullah was far from a friendly man, no matter how much David tried to be his friend. He fed him, housed him, trained him and even saved his life. However, none of that mattered. Abdullah was set in his ways, and the doctor knew why; he missed the *life he once had. Everything was pretty much ripped away from him, and that was a hard pill to swallow. He wore the world on his shoulders and his heart on his sleeves.*

CHAPTER 1

KANGO

"Since you've been away I've been down and lonely
Since you've been away I've been thinkin' of you
Trying to understand, the reason you left me
What were you going thru?
I'm missing you (gangstas need love too)…"
- Master P

Dear Kanon,

    By the time this letter reaches your hands, I'd be long gone. I just wanna say thank you for everything you've done for me, and I could never repay you. I would like to be the first to admit that I'm in love with you—just in case you didn't know. However, I'm sorry I just couldn't do it. It's too much on my poor heart. Kanon, I'm not built for the shit you're built for, and I'm damn sure not built for the pain. I've been through enough growing up. I don't have any room for love. Just in case you're wondering, two detectives came to see me. Don't worry, I ain't say shit. Can't tell what I don't know, right? Right. Well, they had an earful for me, and to be real, I'm not mad at you or Jackie. I'm just disappointed and hurt. Although this was one cold ass winter, I'll always love you. I can't help it. I fell in love with Kanon —not Kango. I have to go, Kanon, but who knows? One day, we may meet again.

    Xoxo… Yours Truly, Fin

For the hundredth time, Kango read Fin's letter, then balled it up yet once again. *She got me fucked up*, he thought to himself, getting up from his bed to head to his car. On the way, he thought of all the things that had transpired over the course of time. The entire plot with his crew was enough to send one into a mental home strapped in a white coat. Jackie Snow had not only gone to jail over a man they thought was solid, but she had also committed murders he knew Enfinity wouldn't forgive them about. Kango had been living reckless, just as Jackie, because not only did he murder Fin's mother, he murdered Lauren. Lauren was Detective Norris' wife, who had locked Jackie away. The killing was gruesome, and Kango prayed that one day he wouldn't be bitten in the ass.

When he pulled up to Jackie's, he was let into a huge gate, then parked his car alongside her Spider. He climbed out and was greeted by Jackie's father, Ace. He knew all about Ace because Calvin Norris, who they thought was Capone, had reached out to him and told him the story about the findings. Calvin thought because he found her father that it would be enough to forgive, but of course, dealing with Jackie, he was a dead man.

"Sup, Ace. Jack here?"

"Kango?" Ace asked, knowing exactly who Kango was.

Kango nodded his head and smiled. He was let into the home, and just in time, he could see Jackie's frame coming down the hall. This was the first time he had encountered Jackie after a few months of her incarceration. Therefore, he stopped and smiled at his dear friend, who was more like a sister. Her stomach wasn't as big as he expected, but she was showing.

"Kangoooo." She smiled brightly and motioned for him to come into her bedroom.

With every step he took, he thought about the day Jackie had got locked up. It was the biggest drop from Cash Lopez of the year, and things didn't go as planned.

"What's up with you, ma? A nigga miss yo' ass." He took a seat on the chaise and rested his arms on his knees.

"I miss you too. Shit been crazy." Jackie shook her head.

"I know, man. What's up with ole' boy?" Kango asked in reference to Capone.

"You already know." Jackie nodded once, and Kango knew exactly what she meant.

"You having a boy." He changed the subject. He wanted so bad to ask the initial question he came to ask, but he didn't wanna seem desperate.

"How do you figure?"

"Your stomach is small and round. Trust me, it's a boy, and you better name him Kango."

They both began to laugh.

"That's a cute name. I just might. So, Kango, what's up? You know I know you like a book, and you here for a reason."

"Damn, a nigga can't check on his big sis?" Kango smirked guiltily.

"Yes, but that dumb ass look on your face tells it all." She matched his smirk, then looked at him with a straight face. "She's at Cash Lopez's house."

"That's all I needed to hear." Kango rushed to his feet and Jackie laughed while shaking her head.

"Kango!" she called out to him before he was completely out the door. When he turned around she said, "...you may just wanna pack yo' shit because we moving to Miami."

A small smile crept upon his face and he only nodded once. "I'll let aunty know." He smiled again and left for his quick trip to Miami.

If this was where he had to relocate to get his girl back, then so be it. He didn't mind a new life. Afterall, his life was with Jackie Snow, so wherever she led, he followed. It was just him and his aunt, so he knew she wouldn't mind. He left Jackie Snow's home feeling so much better. He was gonna pack his things as Jackie insisted, but it would simply have to wait. Right now, he had to get to Fin, so he climbed into his car and headed for the port.

***

After Kango's private jet landed at the Opa Locka Airport, there was a car awaiting his arrival. He climbed inside and instructed the driver to take him to the Lopez estate. He had already spoken to Cash Lopez, but he made sure to tell her not to alert Enfinity. As the car headed for the mansion, Kango couldn't wait to get his hands on her. He understood her pain of finding out all the information the detectives had informed her, but she could have come to him first. In his eyes, a letter wasn't good enough. He needed the proper closure. By God's grace, he wished he could talk to her and plead for her forgiveness. If not, then he would move on, but he still wanted the closure he deserved.

When the car arrived, he watched the house in awe. His home was huge. Even Jackie's mansion was huge, but the Lopez mansion was something like out of a movie. He had never in his lifetime seen a home so big up close. When the huge gate opened, the car pulled inside, and Kango jumped out before the car could come to a halt. He lightly jogged up to the front door, and after knocking, he was greeted by one of Cash's maids. The entire staff was already awaiting his arrival.

"Hola, Senor. Ms. Enfinity, *está aqui*." The older woman motioned for him to follow. She led him down a long hall, then stopped.

Kango counted about eleven doors before they reached the door where Fin could possibly be. He nodded to the polite woman, and before he walked in, he let out a deep sigh. He wasn't sure what he wanted to tell her, but he prayed whatever he would say, would work. After briefing himself for a short moment, he pushed the door open. He stepped further into the room and walked right into the king-sized bed where Enfinity sat with her legs crossed. She had a book in her hands, and she seemed to be in tune with it. When she looked up, her eyes widened as if she had seen a ghost. Her head tilted slightly to the side, and she looked as if the wind had been snatched from her body. Her eyes quickly formed a gloss, and before Kango could utter one word, a lone tear slid down her face in melancholy.

CHAPTER 2

ENFINITY

"Tonight, I'm gonna find a way to make it without you
Tonight, I'm gonna find a way to make it without you
I'm gonna hold on to the times that we had
Tonight, I'm gonna find a way to make it without you..."
-Alicia Keys

"**K**ango." Enfinity spoke his name apprehensively. She couldn't believe the man she had cried over for months, the man she'd told herself she would never encounter again, the man that broke her heart like her father, would not only find her but stand before her as if he craved her touch. The look in his eyes made her want to jump into his arms, but her heart wouldn't let her do it. She had to stand her ground. She began shaking her head from side to side as her body eased out of the bed. She backed up slowly as if he was a stranger that would harm her.

Kango watched her with ease, and with every tear, his heart broke more. He wanted to console her, but he was too afraid of the reaction he might get. Therefore, he watched her closely for a split second. Growing frustrated with the fiasco, he charged for her but came up short. Fin quickly locked herself into the restroom. Kango stood on the other side of the door huffing and puffing as if he was the big bad wolf. Suddenly, he kicked in the door forcefully and snatched Fin up. He pinned her against the wall and had a flashback to the first day he had to get aggressive with her in Jackie's home. It was the first day he tasted her love box and had to yoke her up to let her know who was daddy. It was like déja vu. Only this time, he was here to regain his position in Fin's heart.

"I swear you got me fucked up, Fin. you acting like a nigga gon' hurt you. Like I'm some kind of monster. Enfinity, it's me." He apologetically looked her in the eyes hoping she'd put down her guards and just hear him out.

"You are a monster!" She shoved him hard and tried to run past him, but Kango caught her by the arm and snatched her back into his embrace.

"A nigga loves you. I'm sorry!" He forced her attention. "Fin, I'm sorry!" A tear slid down his face because the cries she began to let out were painful. He held onto her for dear life.

The feeling was too good to Enfinity, but she couldn't. She just couldn't. "Kango, please just go. Please leave me alone." She spoke in between tears. She tried hard to catch her breath, but she couldn't.

"Fin, please, ma." He began rubbing through her hair to try to ease her pain. "Just hear me out. Please, ma? I'm not a monster. I love you, and I'll never intentionally hurt you. You gotta understand, ma, certain things come with my lifestyle. I would never hurt you. It's only two or three people in the world I'll die for, and your one. Fin, I'll give my life for you." Kango spoke repentantly. He meant what he said. He just wished Fin would believe him.

"But you *did* hurt me." She slid from under his grip and walked over to her bed. She laid face down and buried her head into her pillow. She began to weep, and Kango stood back to watch her for a moment. This girl was breaking him down by the seconds. He walked over and took a seat on her bed. The room fell silent because Kango looked for the right words to say. He let out a small sigh and began to pour his heart out.

"Enfinity, Jackie and I aren't monsters, and you know that. You gotta understand, baby girl, everything that happened was before you came around. Once you came into the picture, Jackie and I did our best to protect you. Fin, I bodied your mother because she hurt you. That shit killed me when that bitch did that to you." Kango spoke in reference to the day Enfinity's step-mother stuck her in the neck with a needle that contained heroin. Fin was hospitalized, and that's when she discovered that Jackie had killed both her parents. "I swear on my Aunty, baby girl, Jackie ain't know them were yo' people. I'm not gon' sit here and say it was right, but like I said, had you been in the picture before all this, I'm sure it wouldn't have happened. We would die protecting not only you physically, but your heart. You know I love you, and you know Jackie loves you. Not only Jackie, but Haley as well. You have a family in us." Kango laid his head back on the headboard and closed his eyes.

Again, the room fell silent, and when he felt the bed move, he opened his eyes. Fin was now sitting up and looking at him. She had finally calmed down, but she still had tears in the corner of her eyes.

"I miss Haley." Fin faintly smiled. It warmed Kango's heart, but he didn't get ahead of himself. "I just don't understand how someone can take a woman's life that had children. My mother wasn't a bad person."

"You're right. Just like Haley ain't a bad person, or Maria wasn't a bad person. It comes with territory, ma. This a cold game, and I can't take back what happened, but I could assure you nothing would ever happen again. Especially if it means hurting you."

"I just need some time Kango." She quickly turned her head. Everything he said made sense, but she was torn.

He nodded his head once and got up from the bed defeated. He walked to the door because he was gonna give her the time she requested.

"You got that, but don't take too much time because I ain't going nowhere. As a matter of fact, I'll be moving to Miami soon. Get yo' mind right, baby girl." And with that, Kango walked out of the room, leaving Fin appalled.

She let out a sigh and buried herself back into her pillow. She replayed the event over in her mind, and, again, she began to cry. Only this time, it wasn't because she was afraid. She was torn between life after love. She was in love with Kango, but because she never thought she would see him again, she felt her life was over. However, here he was; in the flesh. Kango was back and had come for what belonged to him. Rather Fin liked it or not, she knew Kango wouldn't give up. Therefore, she prepared herself for the time to come. He was moving to Miami *per* his words, so she knew she had to prepare fast.

***

"So what did he say?"

"He said he was moving out here and soon."

"So what you gon' do? Because from what it seems, that man ain't giving up so easy."

"I don't know. I mean, really, Liyah, it ain't just him; it's his world. I can't get caught up in his lifestyle, and especially with Jackie Snow."

"I understand how you feel. Trust me, I do." Liyah dropped her head. She then looked back up, wondering if she could trust Fin with the information she was about to drop on her. She knew Fin wasn't a rat because Fin explained everything that happened back at the hospital, and she didn't rat on Jackie. "Fin, you gotta promise me you'll never speak on this to no one."

"Pinky swear." Fin raised her pinky finger to lock with Liyah's. When Liyah accepted her finger, they smiled.

"When I was a baby, I was basically dumped off in my car seat to the nearest hospital. My mother was murdered, and that's why I was raised with my grandfather. Basically, he did it out of guilt because he was the reason my mom was killed. Well, to make a long story short, years later, I found out Cash was the one to kill her."

"Nooooo." Fin clutched her mouth, not believing her ears.

"Yep. I never said anything. Not only because it was before my time but because Cash stepped up and raised me as her own. That woman is so genuine. I know it wasn't out of guilt like my grandpa. It could have been because I was her son's girlfriend, but who knows." Liyah shrugged. "However, she started loving me as her own."

"So you forgave her?"

"Yes. I know it sounds crazy, but, yes. I've wanted to ask her only for confirmation, but I let it go. That woman has done everything to right her wrongs. I'm telling you this because maybe you should hear her out. You gotta remember, Fin, Jackie didn't know you when this happened. She may have fallen in love with you before she even discovered it was your mother she killed."

"That's what Kango said," Fin added and dropped her head. It had been a few days since Kango left, and it took everything in her not to reach out. She really didn't know the right words to say, but after the talk with Liyah, she was reconsidering doing so. She really didn't know where she'd begin with Jackie, but eventually, the time would come. Just like she told Kango she needed time, she also needed time with Jackie.

"I gotta figure something out. I don't plan on going back with Jackie, and I don't want your mother taking care of me. It seems like college is over with, so I gotta figure it out." Fin said, trying hard to figure out her life.

It'd been months since she'd lived with Cash Lopez, and Cash took great care of her. She'd treated Fin as if she was her own, but Fin didn't wanna seem like a leach. Although Cash assured her she was good and didn't need anything, she still wanted to contribute.

"I have something up." Liyah smirked with something up her sleeve.

"Oh, Lord, Liyah. What yo' crazy ass got up? I'm with it as long as I won't be in jail."

"We pay the police," Liyah assured her, and she wasn't lying. The entire state of Florida belonged to the Lopez family. They answered to Cash and would dare arrest anyone tied to the cartel.

"Let's do it," Fin replied, watching the coyly look on her face. Whatever the plot was, Fin was down. She was ready to get to it and ASAP.

CHAPTER 3

AALIYAH

"Say that you want me
Say that you'll never leave me
You gotta tell me you need me
Don't let them take your love away..."
- Ashanti

(Previously In Cash Lopez)
The night my Apa was killed by Cash, I didn't regret shit. When I killed Que, I didn't regret shit. When I pulled the trigger on Camery, and sent Monique dumb ass to jail, I didn't regret that shit either. All my life everyone thought that I was the sweet innocent little Liyah, but what they failed to realize, was, I was raised by my grandfather who was the coldest killer in Miami. My entire life involved death. Not one person in my family died from natural causes because every-one died from the hands of another killer, so I had it in me to begin with. I wanted so bad to ask Cash about my mother's death but I chose to leave it alone.

I knew one day the subject would come up and you know what? I wouldn't even be mad at the outcome. I've grown to know the real Cash Lopez and everything she did had a meaning. It didn't take a rocket scientist to know she killed my mom because the demis my grandfather caused. Shit, he killed her whole family. Just because Que blew up the ship physically, Mario ass was behind the hit, so those people's blood was on his hands.

I tried my hardest to stray away from the person that I was now becoming. Because of my son, I didn't want this life but every day it pulled me in. I was trying hard to just focus on my strip club but it was something about the way Cash looked over that stove, that was tempting me. She was really my idol and it felt like I was transforming into her. The stories she had told me, always had my undivided attention. It was like, I wanted to be Cash, and she was now my Ms. Lopez. She, and my grandfather were fucking millionaires due to selling coke. They both sold drugs all over the state and never had a run in with the law. Papi told me I was crazy, but that nigga had his fucking nerves.

True, I loved Papi to death but he had put me through so much; I had a wall up between us. Right now it was all about me and these fantasies of being a Boss Bitch. The thought of selling drugs weighed heavy on me, and It was like I had gotten an adrenaline rush from the murders I committed. So here I am, on a rise to come up. Hey, you never know, I might just be the next Trap Gyrl, or should I say, TRAP PRINCESS (wink).

"**W**hat y'all little crazy girls up to?" Cash peeked her head into Liyah's bedroom door.

Liyah and Enfinity both sat on Liyah's bed with writing tablets and ink pens in front of them. They stopped in midsentence to look over at Cash, hoping she hadn't heard anything they discussed.

"We're getting things ready for school. We're about to check into college."

"That's really good. You too, Fin?" Cash asked, and she nodded yes.

"Okay, great. I'm proud of you guys, and tell that boyfriend of yours I'mma knock his wig back for busting my damn door down." Cash smiled, looking at Liyah. They all laughed because Kango was just crazy. "Well, Kellz and I are going out. Skylar is asleep, and BJ is out."

"Like always. And, okay, Mommy. Y'all have fun." Liyah

faintly smiled.

She was kinda under the weather because BJ was always gone. Now that Cash was back around, he was hustling harder than before. Cash had basically passed her empire to him, so he was heavy in the streets. Had it not been for Fin, Liyah would be lonely as always. Most days, she spent time out shopping, was nestled with a really good book or just chilling around the house with her son. Escolan gave her the peace she needed and kept her occupied. Now that Fin was here, she could get into trouble and be as rebellious as she wanted to be. She still had her close friend, Venicia, but because her and Cali worked things out and were now an item. So she saw less of her.

"Stop looking like that, Liyah," Fin announced. She'd noticed the change in Liyah's attitude. She knew exactly why the sudden sadness because she too had noticed Papi was never home.

"It's nothing." Liyah tried hard to be strong.

"No, it's not. Liyah, I know why you're like this. I mean, it's obvious. And it's okay to be sad. You're a woman, and as women, we want comfort and affection."

"And how do you know so much about love?" Liyah asked with a small smirk.

"Jackie Snow." Fin looked up through a pair of innocent but bubbly eyes. Just the mention of Jackie made her sad. She now had the same for looming look as Liyah. "I watched how Jackie was heavy in the streets. Yes, ruthless, but she wanted to be loved. There was something about Capone I couldn't put my finger on, but I will say he tried hard and he loved her. Jackie was just a bit too much for him. Her lifestyle made him appear lonely, and there was time I would always catch him zoned out as if he missed her.

"The lifestyle everyone around you lives is a crazy one, and I don't see how y'all can do it. Just the short experience I had with Kango was hard." Fin paused thinking about Kango. She looked back up... "He would leave for hours at a time. I would miss him like crazy. I mean, we could be in the middle of something important, and when that phone rang, it was his priority. As much as I hated it, I had to cope with his lifestyle." Fin shrugged as if it was nothing, but each time Kango's phone rang, she would die literally. Not only out of jealousy but worry. She always worried something would happen to him.

"Do you still love him?" Liyah asked, bringing Fin from her daze.

"Yes." She spoke somberly as her eyes began to water, but she refused to cry. "I can't front. I do Liy Liy. I thought that things would get better with time, but when I saw him, it's like my heart collapsed. Every piece of love I had for him came rushing back. I wanted so bad to hate him. I wanted so badly to ignore my feelings, but I can't. It's, like, he cast a love spell on me. For days I've cried, but when he came for me, it helped me understand how he'll fight for me. So it put my heart at peace." For the first time since Fin saw Kango, she smiled.

"Give him a chance, Fin. Don't let love slip away because of someone else's demise. Kango's a good guy, and I've stated that before. He's nothing like Papi. Papi wants to always be the center of attention: the club, the cars, the girls. I know he loves me, and his intentions are never to hurt me, but he has. He's hurt me to the point I lost hope in love. What I'm basically saying is don't give up until he gives you a reason. Be his peace 'cause dealing with Jackie Snow can be a bit much." The girls burst into a fit of laughter breaking the sorrowful moment.

"Huhhhhh." Fin let out a deep sigh and gave what Liyah was saying some thought. She still was unsure, but she knew another encounter with Kango she would break.

"Speaking of the devil." Liyah's Ashanti "Don't Let Them" ringtone began to ring, letting her know it was Papi.

"Hey, Papi." She tried to hide her excitement. After what Fin just said, she was glad he called.

"Sup, big head ass girl. What yo' pretty ass doing?"

"Just chilling with Fin. You good?" Liyah smiled. This was the one thing Papi did to always make her blush bashfully; he would always tell her how beautiful she was.

"Always. I was just seeing what y'all was up to. A nigga finna go up to the club and pick up some dough. I was just letting you know."

"Ugh, a'ight," Liyah replied, rolling her eyes. She hated the club with a passion.

"Man, stop being like that." Papi laughed, but Liyah didn't find shit funny. "What you and Fin been up to, though? Y'all been on some plotting shit lately?" he asked, knowing he wouldn't get a direct answer.

"Boy, mind yo' business," Liyah quickly replied. Because she had the phone on speaker, Fin heard his question and wondered if they had been that obvious.

"Yeah, a'ight. I'll holla at you later, shorty. Love you. Kiss my son."

"Okay. I love you too." Liyah disconnected the line.

"Why we ain't went to the club? I've been here months, and we ain't been once."

"We can go whenever." Liyah shrugged. She wouldn't mind going because this would be an excuse. She'd been plenty of times, but only when Papi invited her. She didn't want to seem like a deranged, insecure baby mama, so she tried hard not to be in Papi's mix.

"Okay, so back to where we were. When are we going to this so-called 'Lab', Liy Liy?"

"Tomorrow." Liyah smirked and pursed her lips.

After tonight, she was ready. Her and Fin were gonna take over the game and become the trap princesses they were. After so much research and help from her white friend, Timothy, she had enough game and clientele to dominate her new hustle.

***

Before the sun could fully beam and Cash Lopez could fully awake, Liyah and Fin were already dressed and ready for their first day of work. Per usual, Papi hadn't come home. Normally, Liyah would have cursed him out, but for the first time, everything fell into place. The moment they climbed into the car, Liyah used her trap phone to call Timothy to make sure he was already up and at the lab. Liyah knew better because Timothy was always up before the roosters crowed, and he did this back when they were in school.

"Ayy, listen, fuck nigga, let me make it clear (Real clear)
It ain't like you made me, pussy nigga,
why you angry? (What the fuck?)
Actin' like you hurt, you showin' way too much emotions
Like a bitch up in a skirt (Bitch), you
steady lyin' like you work..."

Liyah and Fin headed towards the lab rapping the lyrics to Tokyo Jetz's "Heart Breaker." The way Liyah was feeling, the song fit perfectly with her mood. Apparently, Fin was feeling the same way because she sang with meaning. When they arrived at the lab, which was a short drive, they were hype at only 6:19 in the morning. Liyah pulled out her flask and took a swig of 1738, then passed it to Fin. She looked at the flask awkwardly because they hadn't eaten breakfast.

Not wanting to be a Debbie Downer, she took a swig and played like it didn't burn going down. She passed it back to Liyah, and after another swig, they exited the car. Fin watched Liyah with her purse nestled on the cuff of her arm as she knocked on the bar door. She was always so amazed at how Liyah handled life so carefree. She couldn't imagine being in Liyah's shoes for five seconds because it came with obstacles of being not only a Trapstar's wife but a Trap princess. Liyah was a strong individual in Fin's eyes, and in such a short time, she commended her.

When they walked into the lab, Liyah's eyes scanned the room, and she smiled as if she had struck gold. Enfinity looked around not sure what the train track looking tubes consisted of, but she was sure it had something to do with what Liy Liy had up her sleeve. The entire room looked like a science laboratory like out of a movie. There was a small fire pit that sat on each countertop, and it connected to the huge glass filter flask.

"Hey Tim." Liyah hugged the wild hair Caucasian boy, then introduced him to Fin.

He then walked them over to one of the tables and fired up the pit. Another guy, who Fin assumed would be a part of their plot, handed them a pair of lab jackets with face goggles. Timothy began grabbing items and pouring it into the flask. He called out instructions several times so they could remember. The way Tim moved between all four flasks, he looked like a mad scientist.

"We're gonna mix various forms of amphetamine, which is another stimulant drug. We're gonna add another few chemicals to boost its potency. Most common pills for cold remedies are often used as the base for the drugs. I use Tylenol 3 because it helps intense the high." Timothy removed the flask and began examining the contents inside for the right measurements. Satisfied, he placed it back onto the two hundred-sixty degree fire and let it cook further.

Liyah was tuned in, and she pretty much had it from here. Fin, on the other hand, was totally lost. However, Liyah was gonna make sure to help her learn so they could take over the game of Methamphetamine.

CHAPTER 4

BROOKLYN JR. (PAPI)

"Huh? (What?)
Ah, I thought a broke nigga said somethin' (Ah)
Talkin' shit but they still ain't sayin
nothin' (Ain't sayin' nothin')
We gon' trap this bitch out 'til the feds
come (Run it up, run it up)..."
-Moneybagg Yo

(Previously In Cash Lopez)
I never thought in a million years, I would be a father. Liyah had given birth to my first baby boy. Weighing in at 7 pounds and 11 ounces, he was a split image of a nigga. I wanted so bad to name him Brooklyn the third, but because he didn't have my middle name, he wasn't considered a jr. However, we did name him Escolan Brooklyn Carter after my dad and grandpa Esco. Right now he was six months old and already he was getting into shit. He ran around in his walker like the Tasmanian devil. My mom always said he was just like me in many ways, I just prayed he wouldn't be when he got older.

In just these few short years of my existence, I had already seen and experienced too much for a nigga my age. The shit, I've seen, and conquered, I didn't want Lil Sco to have to deal with that shit. Now that we had eliminated all our enemies, I was more than sure we could go on with our lives. My club was doing great and not to mention the money I was investing into Aaliyah's club, we were gonna be straight for the rest of our lives. Liyah had her own dough, but it was my job to cater to her every need. I don't know what it is about her, but it's like she changed overnight.

She had two bodies under her belt and now she was walking around like she was Columbiana or some damn body. Lately I had been contemplating asking her to marry me, but I don't know man, she was moving to a different tune. I mean don't get me wrong, we were happy, and always enjoying life, but something about her was off. In due time, I was gonna pop the question though, because this girl was really my soulmate.

Life was good besides Liyah ole' Griselda Blanco head ass. My moms was happy with her new love life, and my little sister love that nigga Kellz, so that was all that mattered. I felt kinda bad for my aunt, because she was back to square one. I know she was on her fuck niggas tip after Que, but the way Young was checking for her, I don't know, her ass might bite. To be honest, I hope she do because Young was cool ass fuck. It wasn't too many people I trusted, but Young was one. Shit everybody needs love, and I finally realized that.

Even Cali and Venicia were working on their family. At first Venicia wasn't fucking with that nigga, but she finally came around. They had a baby boy also that they named Cali. Right now we all sat by the pool as Kellz Barbecued. Shit been peaceful with my family, and I prayed it would stay like that. I was still the man of these streets, a true Trap Boy by nature, and no one could knock me off my throne.

"Y ou have a collect call from Monique. To accept, dial 5, to block future calls from this facility, dial 9, now."

Pressing 5 on his keypad, Papi sighed, lightly frustrated because the caller wouldn't give up. It had been quite some time since he had spoken to her, and he hoped he wouldn't regret the short call now.

"Hello?" Monique spoke into the phone excited.

The blaring music from the club speakers nearly masked out her voice. Papi put his finger into his free ear to try and drown out the background. "Sup, Moe?"

"I've been calling you. How are you?"

"Shit, I'm straight. A nigga been busy working."

"Oh, okay," she replied sadly.

A small bit of compassion sprained through Papi's veins, so he toned down his sarcasm. "How you holding up in there, shorty?" he asked sincerely.

As much as he wanted to hate Monique, he still felt bad for what happened to her. In their past relationship, Papi actually liked Monique. She was grown, had her own and pretty much had her shit together. Unlike Aaliyah. At the time, Liyah was on some kid shit in Papi's eyes. She had money, but she had to take orders from her grandfather. She couldn't leave the house as she pleased, and when Mario got wind of Papi being alive, he made sure to put a strain on their relationship. He hated Papi with a passion, and it was all because of the hate for Ms. Lopez. Mario and Ms. Lopez were rivals and had been for years. Mario was the one responsible for all the chaos caused in the Lopez's lives. It was just a coincidence Papi had fallen in love with his grand-child. It was also a coincidence Liyah was the daughter of Que.

"I'm okay, I guess. Another few years and I'll be going up for an appeal. That's what I wanted to talk to you about. If you can help me out, I'd appreciate it. I'm not asking for any money, but if you can, could you buy the shop from me? It's hard to maintain, and Ari is having trouble keeping clientele."

"Buy the shop? I might be able to do that. I'll holla at you about it some other time. A nigga kinda busy right now."

"Okay. If you can, thanks."

"You a'ight, ma."

"Papi?"

"Sup?"

"I miss you." Monique spoke nervously.

"A'ight," Papi replied, then disconnected the phone. He slid his phone into his pocket and focused on the atmosphere in front of him.

Tonight he had a packed house. Not only was he here to

pick up his money, but he was also meeting a lady friend. It was nothing serious. He just wanted some head and someone to entertain him while he watched over his establishment.

***

"Damn, shorty. Yo' ass phat as fuck." Papi watched as Mahogany danced on the pole that was located inside of his office.

What started off as a simple date, turned into an audition. When Papi heard Mahogany mention she had just lost her job as a receptionist, he asked her if she knew how to bartend. She replied no, so he asked if she could dance. When she replied yes, this was music to his ears. Papi knew he could use Mahogany in the club because she was sexy. Everyone that worked in his establishment had some sort of sex appeal because it brought in money.

"I mean, I'm not the best, but I could take a few pole lessons." Mahogany jumped down and pulled her Duke shorts from out of her ass.

"Shit, you did good. Real shit, though, you fly. So you gon' get paid, regardless."

"Thank you." Mahogany smiled and took a seat next to him. "Well, I hope you don't look at me as a hoe if I do this," she added nervously.

"Shit, that's yo' business. I can't look at you like nothing because you ain't my bitch." Papi kept it G with her.

Mahogany understood where he was coming from, but it did hurt her feelings because he always made it clear they weren't an item. Mahogany really liked Papi, so she was hoping for more. However, after everything she'd heard about Liyah, she knew she didn't stand a chance in his heart. Liyah wasn't only filthy rich, but she was beautiful and had his child. Mahogany was so obsessed with Liyah, she followed her on Instagram and watched her page daily. Because Liyah wasn't a social media junky, she rarely posted. Mahogany would always be the first to like it, and this was something Papi had no knowledge of.

"Can you wiggle like that with a dick in you?" Papi smirked at Mahogany.

She began laughing, but in her mind, she wanted to scream, *Yes!* "Umm, I guess," she replied shyly.

"Man, come on. You ain't shy. And if you are, you gotta get out of that. You gotta dominate that stage, ma. That's how you gonna eat." Mahogany nodded. "Come here." Papi motioned for her to come over.

When she sat down beside him, she tried to bold because of what he said. Therefore, she tugged at the zipper of his pants, instructing him to unzip them. Papi wasted no time pulling out the monster he had between his legs, and Mahogany's mouth watered. She began jacking him off slowly until he was standing at attention. She then bent down in front of him and wrapped her mouth around the tip. She made sure to get it wet, and when she had covered it in slobber, she went down as far as she could until she gagged.

Mahogany began sucking the life out of Papi's dick, and she did it for so long, her jaws began to tense up. When Papi realized he wasn't going nut from head, he told her to bend over the sofa. She slid out of her shorts, followed by her panties, and bent over, exposing the large tattoo that covered her ass. Papi walked over to his drawer and pulled out a XL Trojan. He slid it onto his dick. Mahogany was still in the same position, and it kept it dick erect. He walked back over to where she stood and opened her ass cheeks to slid inside.

Mahogany bit into her lip and began to let out moans that sounded like tunes. He pushed her head down into the sofa and made her arch her ass. He then clamped onto her waist and began grinding into her hard. The sound of the club's music drowned out Mahogany's screams because anyone that would hear her would think she was being harmed. Papi fucked her hard and good, and he also noticed wasn't shy about her. The way she began throwing her ass back also told him she was a freak. Papi had only known Mahogany a week, so this was the first time he fucked her.

"That's right, ma. Take all that dick."

Papi had to grab her shirt with one hand. Mahogany was throwing it back so wild, Papi stopped and let her take control. He smacked her on the ass a few times, not knowing this turned her on more. She took the initiative to walk over to the pole while he was still inside of her. The pole gave her better leverage, and now she could show Papi what she was working with. She was hoping this would make Papi keep her. But what she didn't know was, pussy was pussy in his eyes, and the best pussy in the world was right at home.

CHAPTER 5

KANGO

*"I was thinkin' that they was, when they really ain't
It's my fault, I can't blame no one
If we take off now, we can catch the sun
Maybe watch it set, have sex, get some rest..."*
- Lil Baby

"So you're leaving for good, huh?"

"Yeah, ma. But I be back."

"No, you're not, Kango. I'm not stupid. You're running to her, huh?" Jamie spoke with so much hurt in her voice.

Kango looked at her, wondering how she knew. He wanted to lie, but he couldn't. Fin had stolen his heart like a thief in the night, and he couldn't front to satisfy Jamie. He anticipated his stay in Miami just to be near Fin. It had been nearly two weeks since the day he last saw her because he and Jackie had to get things in order back in the city. They had to adjust accounts, and spots needed to be rearranged. Now that everything was done, his last stop was to see Jamie, who he had to break the news to. Over a course of time, he had been sleeping with Jamie for pussy. Fin was gone and because his heart wouldn't allow it, he chose to continue smashing Jamie. He had a soft spot for her, but she just didn't do it for him. He needed to be with Fin, and especially after the intense encounter the last time he saw her.

"Man, Jamie, you know what it is."

"I already knew. Ugh..." Jamie rolled her eyes. "Bye, Kanon."

"A'ight." Kango stood to his feet. Normally, he would chastise her for calling him by his government name, but right now he let her ride.

Kango grabbed his keys and dropped a stack of money on the dresser. It was nearly twenty grand, and for the first time, Jamie didn't budge. She was hurt. His money didn't mean shit, and she showed him by getting up and storming out the room. Normally, she would walk him to the door, but, tonight, she was in distress. She headed into the laundry room in the garage and prayed he would just leave. Of course, Kango left without remorse because his heart just wasn't here. He walked out of the home and climbed into his car. He sent Jackie a text to let her know he was on his way to the private jet. His entire life had already been hauled out, which consisted of a few clothing, his jewelry, and his money that was in the safe—located in he and his aunts mansion.

Everything else was left behind to the new tenants he rented the home to. Because it was his first mansion, and with his aunt, he loved the home dearly. So he refused to sell it. Tonight was gonna be a big change for Kango after years of his life. Never in his wildest dreams had he ever thought of leaving Cali. However, for Fin and Jackie, he was willing. Other than Fin, he knew because of Cash Lopez he was gonna make a drastic change. Cash had things on lock, and the entire state belonged to her. Fuck the state, the ocean was hers. Cash was Jackie's supplier, and because she was like the female version of the great El Chapo, he knew it was bigger than Jackie. He prepared himself mentally and drove the rented car for the port.

***

The entire ride to the port, Kango looked down to the small black velvet box that contained a quarter-million diamond ring. He contemplated with himself about asking Fin to carry his last name. He wasn't gonna ask right away, but he was saving it for when the time was right. Kango couldn't wait to get to the Lopez estate because this time, things would be different. He was gonna make love to Fin and make her retract her attitude towards him. Every day he spent away from her made him crave her more. After the last encounter with Jamie was when he decided to go along with the proposal. Jamie was a cool chick, but he didn't see a future with her. He needed someone he could plant a few seeds in—someone that was pure, and that someone was Fin.

When the car pulled up to the port, Kango exited, dressed simply in a white tee and jeans. However, his thirty thousand dollar trench coat moved viciously because of the 9 millimeter that hung inside of the pockets. He held one on each side because he moved cautiously in the cold streets. His hair was neatly twisted in four plaits, that social media referred to as Pop Smoke braids. Kango knew he was that nigga, so whenever he moved, he held not only confidence, but a cocky demeanor that swooned women in. This time around, if Enfinity rejected him, he would just move on. Mami was filled with women that would bow down at his feet. His name alone spoke volumes and because he had visited the city frequently, the ladies knew exactly who the *Cali God* was. His name held weight right along with Jackie Snow. He was well paid and would put a bullet into whoever crossed him.

He let out a deep sigh as he boarded the jet, and when his eyes fell onto his aunt Jean, he smiled. Aunt Jean was in the back wrapped into a throw blanket. When she saw that her nephew had arrived, she matched his smile excitedly. Jean was ready for the major change and because she knew there was a love story awaiting for her favorite guy in the world, she was ready for the transition. Kango headed up the jet aisle and took a seat across from his aunt. He removed his coat, and his aunt looked at the guns he carried and smiled. She understood his lifestyle, and she respected him to the utmost.

Jean was a hood chick back in her days, and she was devotedly in love with Simon, the head of his own organization. She understood what it was like to be in love at a young age, and she also understood the extreme of protection was important. She knew that Kango only loved his money, but after witnessing the love that Enfinity brought to the table meant more than a dollar. Kango hadn't told his aunt about the ring he copped because he wanted it to be a surprise. He knew how much she loved Fin, and as long as he had the best lady in the world on board, he was content.

After a few minutes of waiting, Jackie Snow's limousine had pulled into the port along with a few of her guards. Kango anxiously smiled because it was time. He watched Jackie through the window as she exited the car and made her way to the jet. He couldn't help but smile because she, too, was dressed comfortably, but she had on a long fur coat that he knew cost a fortune. When she climbed onto the jet, the first thing he saw was her stomach. Jackie was glowing, and although she had been through hell these last few months, she was smiling.

Moments later, Ace walked onto the jet holding a sleeping, Haley. Kango stood to his feet and waited for him to lay the baby down. Once he came back to the front, Kango gave him a manly hug. Jackie sat next to aunty and Ace sat beside Kango with his newspaper. The pilot approached the group and handed them a bottle of Ace. Kango stood to his feet and grabbed a few glasses. He passed one to Aunt Jean, then Ace.

"This is to a new life." Kango popped the bottle and they all began to clap.

Jackie was mad because she couldn't drink, but she still was excited. "A new life!" Jackie added, and, again, they all cheered.

The pilot powered on the plane and began adjusting for takeoff. Everyone indulged in a conversation of what they were gonna do as soon as they landed. Kango was ready to see his girl, Jackie was ready to sleep, Jean just wanted to see their new home, and Ace was ready to see Cash Lopez's fine *ass* as he called her. Jackie had already purchased a brand new sixteen bedroom mansion for all of them to stay in. She knew, eventually, Kango and Jean would move out, but for now, they were all gonna be a family.

CHAPTER 6

CASH LOPEZ

"Hit me like a ray of sun
Burning through my darkest night
You're the only one that I want
Think I'm addicted to your light..."
- Beyoncé

(Previously In Cash Lopez)
"Boyyyyy" this has been a long year. A good one but long. I had the best man God could give me, well next to Brooklyn Nino. Can't no man on earth take Brook's place and I'm sure they all knew that. Kellz was good to me though and with him I was secure. It was like, I was the storm because of all the things I've been through, and he was my calm. The day he chose me over a woman he had been with since school, proved to me he was the one. He had finally gotten a divorce, and to my surprise his ex-wife wasn't tripping. She let her kids come over on the weekends, and although we didn't speak, she wasn't a pain in my ass.

A few times Kellz had mentioned kids, but no way was I bringing another baby into this world. I had Lil Esco and Lil Cali so I was good on kids. Lil Esco was a handful. I swear he was like another reincarnated BJ. At only six months, this little boy got into everything. Ever since his mom had killed Camery and Que, her ass was on some gangsta shit. It was really crazy because she reminded me so much of myself. However, I pray she didn't follow in my footsteps.

Lately she had been asking me all kinds of questions about killing and drugs, and that was a sign of interest. Lord have mercy.

Braxton and I had finally come to terms because of our child.

I made sure to take Sky to see him monthly because I wanted them to keep the bond they always had. I asked him plenty of times to move down to Miami but he would always refuse. A few times I had gone to visit, I slept with him out of guilt. One drunk night, and heavy thoughts, led me into his bed; I just prayed he would never tell on me. I loved Kellz so much. If Braxton told, I would probably kill him. I couldn't, and I refused to lose Kelly. Kelly and I were opening a movie theater and it was the best idea yet. When he decided to name it after Brooklyn, that shit warmed my heart. I know deep down inside he didn't mean for us to fall in love but who better than the only man Brooklyn trusted that would keep me secure.

Life was great due to all my enemies being eliminated. Mario was finally gone, and the nigga that I always thought I could trust, was now dead and gone. I couldn't believe Que. This whole time he was the one that set my mom up to go to jail. I could just imagine she's prolly rolling over in her grave. The nigga even worked with Mike, now that's even crazier. I think it hurt me more to know he was a snitch. Even more than knowing he was behind the explosion. If it was one thing I hated, and that was a fucking rat. I hated I couldn't be the one to kill him, but knowing his own flesh and blood pulled the trigger, was the satisfaction I needed.

When I was taken down to the station, they questioned me about Que being murdered. Of course when I gave them my name, I was quickly released. They ruled the murder as, trespassing and self-defense, especially because BJ was shot and on his own yacht. Last night I had a long talk with Liyah and she looked like she wanted to ask me something. I was more than sure it was the question she's been dying to ask. Did I kill her mother? For some odd reason she didn't ask, but when she did, I was gonna be truthful.

Well y'all, it's been a long ride and guess what? Cash muthafucking Lopez is back in the flesh and still the baddest bitch around. My whip game still cold over the stove and I got the purest shit on the streets. You damn right, I copped three hundred birds and, THE BITCH IS BACK! Grade A Trap Gyrl

"**B**aby, why we never go to the movies?"

"Because we own the movies, Kelly."

"Exactly. So, again, why we never go?"

"You wanna go to the movies?"

"Yeah. I wanna take you out on a normal date like normal people." Kellz wrapped his arms around Cash's waist and kissed into the nape of her neck.

"Okaaaay," Cash cooed then kissed the side of his face. "What we gon' see?"

"Let's check out that *Halo* movie."

"Yes, I wanna see that. I saw the preview, and it looks good."

"A'ight well go grab yo' purse. I'mma go tell Maggie to watch Sky, since her sister and cousin are always so busy now." Kellz smirked, referring to Liyah and Fin.

"They've enrolled into school. I'm so proud of them." Cash smiled, not knowing school was the last thing on their roster.

Kellz looked on but didn't give his input. He was no fool. Something was up with the two, and he could tell by the dark circles forming underneath their eyes. Every day, they came home like they were worn out, and Kellz always took notice. He would never speak on it because he didn't want to alert Cash, however, he knew one day they would be exposed.

After securing Skylar and getting things situated around the home, Cash and Kellz headed out to begin their night out in the town. Cash complained about going out to eat first, but Kellz told her no. They were gonna eat popcorn and nachos. Finally agreeing, Cash sat back in her seat and grabbed Kellz's hand as she normally did. Like always, he squeezed it, then kissed the back of it. She'd blush fondly. Kellz and Cash had an old school love with sparks flying like 4th of July. They made out like two teenagers in high school, and their love kept them young. Cash couldn't wait until they were inside of their theater so she could snuggle against him. The two were inseparable.

With everything Cash had been through in her life, she chose to never leave his side. After the horrific death of Brooklyn Nino, she worried about Kellz. In fear of something happening to him, she let her sons, BJ and Young, take over her empire. Kellz, who kept a low profile, would be tested in the streets, and she couldn't risk it. Mario was dead, Que was dead, but in this game, you never knew who would come gunning.

"Come on, ma. Get yo' pretty ass out." Kellz opened Cash's door.

When Cash stepped out of the car, she smiled and thanked him. The moment she turned to look at the huge sign that read Brooklyn Cinema, her heart instantly fluttered. She was proud of her establishment, and the name alone was endearing.

The few guards that were with Cash and Kellz surrounded them, then escorted them inside. Cash had forgotten all about her guards because she had grown tired of always being watched. Just like her mother, Ms. Lopez would always make her take detail wherever she went, and Kellz was the same way. Cash knew her safety was important, but she often dreamed about living a normal life. With her purse snuggled on the fold of her arm, Cash nuzzled into Kellz with her free hand. When they stepped into the theater, the bright lights beamed, and the entire staff stopped to look. Everyone began to chatter, and some scattered around to make sure they looked busy. When the Manger, Javier, noticed the two, he quickly ran from around the counter to greet them.

"Ms. Lopez." Javier kissed Cash's hand. He then nodded to Kellz excited.

"Javier, are there any theaters empty?"

"Yes, sir. We just cleaned out theater 8."

"Okay. Well, we wanna see *Halo*. Also, send us some popcorn, nachos, two Cokes and some red vines," Kellz ordered because he knew red vines were Cash's favorite.

"And a pretzel with jalapeno cheese."

"Pretzel?" Kellz asked, because he knew she wasn't gonna eat all that food.

"Yes. I want a pretzel." Cash poked out her lip.

"A'ight big ass baby. Let me find out you prego," Kellz shot from the side of his eye.

"That's out. You know I ain't letting that happen." Cash grabbed Kellz's hand and pulled him towards the theater. His feelings were a bit hurt because no matter what, Cash just wouldn't give him a baby. He didn't understand why. She gave Nino and Braxton a child, but she wouldn't give him one. She always said they had enough kids, and she made sure to take her birth control faithfully. At one point, she began getting Depo shots, but it blew her up, so she switched to the pill. Although Kellz was the perfect father, there was something holding her back.

Stepping into the theater, Cash and Kellz decided to sit in the middle of the theater. The guards posted up by the door, and the staff made sure to exit from above on the second level. They began to make small talk while the previews played. Just before the movie came on, the attendant pushed a cart inside with their food. Cash wasted no time diving into her pretzel, and just like she knew, Kellz wanted a bite. She fed Kellz the pretzel, then playfully rubbed cheese on the tip of his nose.

"Oh, you wanna play?" Kellz snatched her up, and she fell into his lap in a fit of laughter. "Lick it off," he demanded, making her laugh harder. "Lick it off, ma." Kellz licked his lips sexually, and that gesture turned Cash on.

She licked the cheese off of his nose, then placed a kiss on his lips. The theater went dark letting them know the movie was about to begin, so they sat back on the recliner chair and tuned in.

Cash watched the introduction, and it was beautiful. When Ace Hood appeared on the screen, she smiled. He was a sexy dread head just like she liked them, and his body was to die for.

"Get fucked up." Kellz smirked, noticing the gleam in her eyes.

Cash looked over knowing she was caught, however, she just smiled and focused back on the screen. She grabbed Kellz's hand for assurance, then kissed it, just as he always did her.

Halfway through the movie, Cash was forlorn in a zone. There was something about the movie that was just too damn familiar. It was an endearing love story, but there was something she couldn't quite put her finger on. Throughout many scenes, Cash and Kellz would look over at one another beyond belief. Apparently, they both were thinking the same thing, but neither of them spoke upon it. The main female character was a ruthless drug lord. Her father went to a federal prison and left her an empire. She fell in love with a dread head, which was Ace Hood, but the trip part that got her was, the girl owned a club and a beauty bar.

As the movie went along, Cash had tears in her eyes because it was, indeed, a great love story. Everything about the two main characters was so overwhelming Cash watched with tears coating the rim of her eyes. Ace proposed to the girl, and they had begun to plan a really big wedding. From time to time, Kellz would sneak a peek at Cash, and his face would ball up in knots, jealous. He knew the movie reminded her of Nino, and because of the tears, he sat there dismal.

When the movie had come to the near end, a wedding began to take place that had Cash unsettled in her seat. The bride looked really beautiful as she made her way towards the groom. The setting was on a beautiful beach, and the sound of waves crashing against shore could be vividly heard in the background. After exchanging vows and a memorable kiss, they grabbed each other's hand to run off towards the crowd. Suddenly, an explosion occurred, and Cash jumped to her feet as if she was there. She clutched her mouth with a stream of tears pouring down her face. She looked over at Kellz, and he too was blown back by the ending. Cash continued to watch the screen in a daze, and when she saw the name of the executive producer, she made a mental note of it.

She turned to grab her purse, and without another word, she headed for the car a bit shaken. She was so astounded she didn't bother to grab Kellz's hand as she normally did. He noticed but he let it ride. His heart was aching because he knew she was thinking of his homie, but just like any other time, he left it alone. Often, he would catch Cash gazing at pictures and falling into a memorable daze. Because he knew he couldn't compete, he would turn the other cheek. Cash would never love another man as she loved Nino, so stressing himself out was a waste of time. He had to take it to the chin and keep his head up. She loved Kellz dearly, but the fact remained, he wasn't Brooklyn Carter.

CHAPTER 7

DOCTOR STINE

*"They say that time's supposed to heal ya
But I ain't done much healing..."*
- Adele

"Oh my God, Abdullah, it's sooo big! It's sooo...ohhhh shit...He could never make me feel like this. Yes, sweetheart, don't stop. Ohhh, yes!"

"Then why you keep running? Bring that ass here."

"It's too big. I can't take it...ohhh, shit, but it feels so good."

"You a big girl. You can take it all. Ohh, shit, I'm abou...I'm about to nut."

"Can I cum?" Charlotte asked for permission to release her nut.

"Cum on this muthafucka."

"Urgggggg...it's coming! It's comin...Oh my God...it's..."

Just as Abdullah was releasing his nut for the second time tonight, the sound of the Siberian Husky began to bark as he did every time headlights flashed in the yard.

"He's here." Charlotte Stine quickly raced to her feet.

Abdullah tucked his semi-hard dick into his sweats and left the room. He headed down the hall for his bedroom and went into the restroom to clean himself off.

Outside, Doctor Stine listened to his wife's pleasurable

cries, and a smile crept upon his face. He pushed pause on the headset that was connected to a recording monitor inside of the home, satisfied with yet another part of content. For years, he had been listening to his undevoted wife scream out in ecstasy as Abdullah pulverized her pussy. The same pussy that'd belonged to Doctor Stine for nearly two decades. He was surprised that Charlotte had been cheating because he never had to deal with infidelity. However, she reminded him of the Adam and Eve story from the Bible. Eve bit the apple, which was forbidden, and that's exactly who Abdullah was: the apple. When he stepped out of the car, he headed for the door slowly to give them time to clean up. He would hate to catch them in the act because his plan would be ruined.

"Honey?" he called out to his wife, and within seconds, she came flowing down the hall.

She was now wearing a long grey gown and her robe. Her hair was pinned up, and she wore a smile as if she was happy to him.

"Hey, love. I've missed you." She kissed him on the lips, using the same mouth she had done Lord knows what with.

"I've missed you too. Long day at work." Doctor Stine took her face into both hands and kissed her forehead. "What did you cook?"

"I made steak, greens I picked from the yard, and jasmine rice. Are you hungry?"

"Sure. I'm gonna go wash up. By then, you'll have my plate ready."

"Okay."

Doctor Stine headed up the hall for his bedroom, and just as he made it, Abdullah was coming out of the restroom. He kept his head straight until Doctor Stine spoke.

"Hey, there, buddy."

"Sup." Abdullah kept it short and moved along to his bedroom.

Doctor Stine was used to it, so he went into his room and prepared for his shower. He found it amusing that he had saved the man's life, but it didn't mean a thing. Since the day Abdullah had awakened, he wouldn't utter a word. As years went by, and he had begun to recover, it was still the same results. He spent countless years locked away in his bedroom like some sort of caveman. He would only come out to work out, eat and shower.

On many occasions, Doctor Stine would try to hold conversations with him, but he always kept things short and simple. He was in a shell that only consisted of himself. He wasn't shy by far. He just didn't care to indulge with the world. He was a heart broken man that felt like he had no reason to live. He wanted to ask many times why didn't Doctor Stine just let him die? He didn't want to be on this earth, and nothing could make him change his mind. No money, no sex from Charlotte, and damn sure not a man who he felt had a motive.

CHAPTER 8

ENFINITY

"How did you get in
Nobody's supposed to be here
I've tried that love thing for the last time
My heart says no, no..."
- Deborah Cox

E nfinity's phone rang just as she was about to pour the Tylenol into the flask. She looked over, and when she didn't recognize the number, she ignored it. When it began to ring a second time, she dried her hands on the towel and answered. "Who's this?"

"Where the fuck you at, yo'?" Kango's voice blared through the phone.

Fin's heart instantly melted, and a sense of nervousness shot throughout her body. "I'm...I'm...I'm at school, Kanon," Fin lied, looking down at the flask in front of her.

There was well over ten grand alone in the utensil, which made her more timid. She then looked at Liyah, who was across the warehouse but couldn't hear a word. Liyah was busy measuring and mastering her new craft. Her goggles were nestled over her eyes, and she was bopping her head to Lil Baby's *My Turn* Album.

"And what school is this?"

"Umm, uh, Dade," she rushed. She really wasn't lying, in a

sense. She had enrolled in school; she just didn't attend.

"Yeah, a'ight, ma. Bring yo' ass straight home."

"For what, Kango? And why you at my house?"

"Man, don't question me. And this ain't yo' crib no more. We got another house, but I'mma let you live for a while."

Fin smacked her lips trying hard to act unfazed, but knowing Kango was in Miami tugged at her heart strings. "Hello? Hellooo?" Fin called out to Kango, but he had already disconnected the line.

"Why you over here looking like that?" Liyah walked up and asked. She was done with her work for the day, so if Fin needed help, she was gonna help so they could head home and get some rest.

Every day, Liyah and Fin had been leaving the house like they were really going to school. They spent countless nights counting money from their sales and saturated mornings in the warehouse cooking. It had been twenty sleepless nights so far, but with the way the money was pouring in, Fin didn't mind. It felt good to know she was on a team of winners. She didn't have to worry about the law, and most importantly, she could purchase anything she desired without the sympathetic help from Jackie Snow. Enfinity still wanted to open her lash bar, and already, seven days of sales she had accumulated enough.

"Kango," Fin replied unbothered. However, she was, indeed, bothered.

"They're here." Liyah already knew what she meant.

Fin nodded her head but didn't utter a word.

Liyah picked up on her nervousness, so she searched for words to make her stay afloat. "Fin, don't let him get to you. Keep your game face on. You love him, and he loves you dearly, but take things slow so you don't overwhelm yourself. Plus, we don't need any distractions right now." Liyah knew exactly how things would pan out. She knew with love came a distraction that neither of them needed. She knew of Fin's goals and she wanted her to execute them.

"Nah, I'm good." Fin tried hard to mask what she already

knew; Kango was back, and he was gonna interfere with her hustle. He was not only jealous but very egotistic. He was gonna block her every move and demand her attention.

"Well, I'm done. Let me help you so we can go deal with that crazy man of yours." Liyah moved towards the flask next to the one being occupied and began helping Fin with her last ounce.

"That's not my man."

"And who you tryna convince? Me or yourself?" Liyah smirked, making Fin laugh.

They both shared a laugh and then began preparing for what was ahead. At this point, Fin knew she wouldn't be getting any rest because her blood was flowing with anxiety.

***

When Fin and Liyah entered the home, Cash was seated on the sofa with her laptop. She looked up as she noticed the girls coming through the door. She faintly smiled, and something about the way she looked tugged at Fin's heart. Since Fin had been in Miami living in Cash's mansion, she and Cash built a bond. She loved Cash, and no matter the stories she had heard, she never let it cloud her judgement. Over the course of time, everyone spoke upon Cash Lopez. They painted this picture of her as if she was some ruthless killer. However, that wasn't the case. Cash was sweet with a big heart, and no matter what, she always put her family first. She was the ideal mother, unlike Jackie Snow. Money was more important to Jackie than her child, and her love life, so Fin knew she didn't stand a chance. The short time she'd lived with Jackie, she took a liking to her as well, but after everything she learned, she felt it was all fake love.

"How was school?" Cash asked, sitting her laptop down beside her. She picked up a cup of coffee and took a sip.

"It was good," Liyah quickly replied.

"How was the movie, Ms. Cash?" Fin asked, quickly changing the subject. She took a seat across from her. Liyah continued on towards the back of the home to check on her son.

"It was really good." Cash looked off into the air, and Fin quickly picked up on the sudden mood change. "Your man is here." Cash did the same by quickly changing the subject of the movie.

Hearing Cash mention *her man* made Fin's heart sink. It was like right on cue, she looked up, and his aroma had begun to linger.

"He's here?" Fin spoke pensively above a whisper. Her eyes grew wide the moment Kango came into view. Like always, that electric volt ran through Fin's body, colliding with the rapid pump of her heart.

"Daddy's home." Kango cockily spoke in his heavy NY accent.

Fin nervously brushed a strand of her wild mane from her face and tucked it behind her ear. Their eyes danced with one another, and it was like the entire room stopped.

"Well, hello." The sound of Jackie Snow's voice brought Fin from a silent stare down battle with Kango. Her face instantly sank into a frown until Haley's energy blessed the room.

"Enfinityyyy!" Haley ran full speed into Fin's arms. She used this as a way to buy time so she wouldn't have to make eye contact with Jackie.

"I missed you, little girl." Fin smiled at the pretty young girl, but her heart continued to rapidly pump inside of her chest. Between both Jackie and Kango being present, it was a battle that consisted of two against one.

"Let me holla at you, Fin," Kango demanded more than asking.

"I'll be right back, baby," Fin told Haley with a subtle smile. Although she was nervous all hell, she was happy Kango was rescuing her from Jackie's presence. She stood to her feet and followed Kango towards the back of the home.

"Kango, yo' ass bust down any more muthafucking doors, I'mma beat yo' ass myself," Cash spoke, making everyone laugh but Jackie.

Fin could feel Jackie watching her as she made her way pass, but she refused to look in her direction. However, she did notice the small, round stomach Jackie produced.

When Fin and Kango made it outdoors, Fin let out a deep sigh to settle her mood. The sun had now blossomed, and it was a beautiful day in Miami. Everything about Cash's yard was a perfect setting, and especially the huge waterfall that sat in the middle of the yard. Taking a long stroll through the huge yard, Kango stopped near the pool and decided to sit there. There was a brief silence between the two, so the sound of the hummingbirds echoed through the air. Kango tried to gather the right words, and Fin was gathering her rebuttals for anything he asked.

"So how was school?" he asked, not knowing what else to say.

The entire way to Cash's mansion, Kango had a million things to say, but now in Fin's presence, he was lost for words. Flashbacks of their last encounter vividly played in his mind, and he felt better because she didn't have that same pool of tears pouring down her face. He hated to see Fin cry, and especially if he was the one causing it. Each time he let her down, he felt ten times worse because he was the one that was supposed to bring her peace and joy.

"It was cool."

"That's what's up. I'm proud of you, ma."

"Thank you." She flashed a short smile. "So you're here for good?"

"Fin, I told you I was coming to stay. Jackie was ready to leave Cali."

"Oh. Okay. Where' Uncle Capone?" she asked, and Kango took a moment to reply.

He really didn't know what to say because of the circumstances. Fin already looked at them as monsters, so he was a bit nervous to admit Capone was dead. "Dead." Kango finally admitted. Fins head titled in shock, and her heart went out to Capone.

"He was a cop all along," Kango added before she jumped to conclusions.

"A cop?" She covered her mouth as it hung on the floor.

Kango nodded instead of going fully into details.

Capone being dead didn't surprise her, however, him being a cop explained a lot. "That's crazy. So all along..." she went to speak but couldn't finish her statement.

"Nigga was a fucking pig, snaking us." Kango shook his head.

He actually liked Capone at one point—up until he received the call from Jackie. Jackie hadn't been booked in when she placed the call. Because she was so connected, she was given an untraceable cellular phone to make the call. After telling Kango about Capone, she instructed him to kill Lauren, which was Capone's wife. At the time, Lauren had left Capone for another cop on the force, but Jackie still wanted her dead. "Fuck all that, Fin. You coming home with me?" Kango asked, but Fin remained quiet.

"I don't know, Kango. I mean, not only Jackie, but us. I still need some time." Fin spoke apprehensively, too scared to look at him.

"So what if I told you I wanted to make you my wife?" Kango pulled the ring from his pocket. He wanted to do an entirely different proposal, but Fin was making him feel like he had to rush.

Enfinity looked over the ring, and it was beautiful. Her heart was screaming, yes, but her mind was clouded with doubt. "I don't know, Kango." She dropped her head.

"A'ight." Kango stood to his feet. He didn't get the response he was looking for, so there was nothing left to say.

Fin watched Kango until he disappeared into the home. She wanted so bad to call out to him, but his facial expression made her second guess. She didn't wanna forgive him so easily, and she damn sure didn't want to move in with Jackie. She knew sooner or later she would have to face her, but at this moment, she just wasn't ready.

CHAPTER 9

BROOKLYN JR. (PAPI)

"We can't never let'em break our mind
We gotta stay strong
Conquer and don't divide
I come at peace, my heart already set on fire…"
- Lil Baby

"Sup, baby girl? How was school?"

"Good. I got an A on my first test," Liyah lied. She began re-twisting Escolan's loc's, hoping Papi didn't pry further.

"That's what's up. What you taking up anyway?"

"All kinds of classes, BJ. Why?"

"Shit, just asking. I really don't understand why you going to school, anyway."

"For an education, nigga."

"For what? It's pointless because you got mils, Liy Liy. Hell, billions with my bread combined. Let me find out you just wanna get away from us." Papi smirked then dropped to his knees so he could play with his son. He grabbed one of Escolan's locs and examined the length. His hair had finally locked up and was hanging down his shoulder. He tripped off how much his son looked like him, and especially with the same hairstyle that he wore.

"I never wanna leave my baby."

"Damn, what about me?" Papi dropped his lip as if he was sad.

"Well, you're never here." Liyah stopped twisting and looked at him.

He didn't know what to say because it was true. Therefore, he grabbed the remote and powered on the television. From the corner of his eyes, Papi could feel Liyah watching him. He knew what she was thinking, and he hoped she didn't start tripping. He himself knew he was moving fast in the streets, but he had to run his mother's empire. He couldn't let Cash continue to risk her life on the streets, so it was his duty to protect his mother. Over the course of time, Papi had formed a small crew along with the crew of niggas Cash had handpicked herself. His main two were Goon and Peezy because they had gained his trust and proved their loyalty.

He and Goon were much closer because Peezy had a family. Peezy was more of the family type that just wanted to provide. However, Goon was more like Papi: levelheaded but wild. He kept a pistol and would kill anybody that crossed his empire. He was glad he had met Papi because niggas like him only came a dime a dozen. Goon had a major clientele established, but once he became part of Papi's, team his money grew along with his empire. Papi was more of Goon's supplier because he had his own traps set up across Miami.

Papi turned to look at Liyah, who was still watching him. He couldn't help his wandering eyes because she was wearing a small gown. Her legs were crossed, one over the other, and because of the short gown, he could see right between her legs. His dick instantly grew in his pants, and when he noticed Lil' Esco had fallen asleep, he was ready to make his move.

"Lay him down," he demanded, and Liyah looked at him as if he was crazy.

She was in her feelings, but Papi didn't care at the moment. It had been a couple weeks since they made love, therefore, he had to feel inside of her. He stripped out of his clothing because he knew Liyah wouldn't resist. With one hand, he began to stroke himself, and with the other, he grabbed the remote and turned to YouTube.

He wanted Liyah to listen to the lyrics of Lil Baby's "Catch The Sun" song. He and Kango had agreed that the song was a hit, and it made perfectly good sense. They wanted to catch the sun with their women before things were too late. Well, for Kango, they might have been because he explained how Fin turned down his proposal. This made him wonder if Liyah would one day give up on him and fall out of love.

Liyah took the baby into his bedroom and returned eagerly. She couldn't front if she wanted too; she needed to get laid and had been fiending for Papi's touch since the last time they had sex. When she walked back into the room, Papi was laying on the bed fully naked. His body was so sexy, and the tattoos that flourished him only added to his sex appeal. He was stroking his long dick as he watched Liyah with hunger. She stripped out of her clothing and laid next to him. Papi didn't make a move right away. Instead, he continued to stroke himself as the lyrics played in the background. Liyah took notice of the song and smiled inside.

When the song went off, Papi turned to his side and enchantingly looked her in the eyes. "You see this muthafucka, Liy Liy?" he referred to the monster between his legs. When Liyah looked down, a throb between her legs appeared. "Can't no bitch make it rise like you, ma, so get them thoughts out yo' head. Come here." He pulled her body on top of his.

Liyah landed right on top of him perfectly. Papi watched her perky breasts that sat up without a bra. Because she had breast fed Escolan his first eight months, her breasts still stood firm. He traced her body with the back of his two fingers admiring everything about her. Her skin was flawless, her body was banging, she had the most prettiest face God could create and her pussy was tight and warm.

Papi lifted her body slightly and inserted himself inside. As Liyah went down, her pussy gripped his dick all the way down.

"Damnnnn." Papi frowned blissfully knowing it wouldn't be long before he reached a peak higher than Mount Rushmore.

Liyah bent the top of her body down and began bouncing her ass on the tip of his stick. She began rotating her bottom as she looked Papi in the eyes. Papi bit into his bottom lip as he smashed into her.

"Papiiii, shittt, baby!" Liyah screamed out but not missing a beat. With one hand, she tugged into her lengthy hair. Her wild side always turned Papi on. It was like she always turned into his little porn star.

Her pussy had him gone.

"Liy Liy, this pussy good as fuck. Damn, ma, this pussy good. Ride that muthafucka!" He slapped her on the ass.

She continued to make her ass clap as she bounded up and down only using her lower body. After nearly thirty minutes, they changed positions and ended up on the dresser. Liyah cocked her legs open, and Papi positioned himself in between. He wrapped his arms under Liyah's armpits to latch onto her. He used this method to pound inside of her and pull her down every time he went into her.

"You love me?"

"I'm in love with youuuuu…shit, Papi."

"You ain't never leaving me?"

"Papi, just fuck me, baby. Ohhhh, shit, just fuck yo' pussy, daddy."

That's all Papi needed to hear. Liyah knew he was a beast, and she also knew what turned him on. She wanted to be fucked hard because it had been so long her body desired him. Papi got a little more aggressive by laying Liyah down and knocking over all the contents on the dresser. When he had her pinned down, and could feel his whole dick being swallowed inside of her, he laid his body down on top of her and began kissing her. Their kiss was wet and intense. Their love was over the edge, which made their sex more memorable. Sex was one of the things that kept their connection alive. Sooner or later, Papi would be putting his daughter inside of her, then after, he would make her his wife.

CHAPTER 10

CASH LOPEZ

"But don't make me close one more door,
I don't wanna hurt anymore
Stay in my arms if you dare, Or must I imagine you there
Don't walk away from me, I have nothing, nothing, nothing
If I don't have you..."
- Whitney Houston

S tanding on the balcony of her bedroom, Cash Lopez gazed
out into the sun that had just set. The sky had her tran-
quilized and equally fed her mind that had been consumed with scenes from the motion picture. Since the day
of the movie, Cash had been disconsolate. The movie brought
back so many memories of her and Nino's love. Not only that,
but how her mother, father and friends lost their lives on the
ship. Cash knew that either someone close to her had to partake
in the filming, or someone was overly creative. For hours in the
day, she had been researching the man that not only executive
produced it but also directed the movie. So far in her discoverance, she found out about a seminar that was being hosted by
him and a team of medical staff. The event was due to take place
in four days, and Cash was gonna show up in hopes to see the
man and get some answers.

When it came to Cash's life and the events that had taken
place, she didn't toy around. Money was the last thing on her

mind. Therefore, he would have to pay with his life. From the day of the explosion, Cash has been living in pure hell, which would be an understatement. Hell couldn't be as bad. Her heart was broken, and although she tried hard to mask the pain of losing her parents every day, she felt she wasn't living. She tried to be strong for not only her children, but Kellz as well. She'd spent countless days crying her eyes out when no one was around. They said time healed all wounds, but the scars from that day would forever hurt.

The sound of the door slowly opening made Cash quickly turn around. She looked into the eyes of the man she knew she put through enough pain. Kellz stood by the door, and like always, he wore a worried look. For days, he'd asked Cash was she okay, and she would reply, *yes*. However, Kellz knew she wasn't okay by far. He asked numerous times if she wanted to talk about it, and she would always say, *no*. Kellz gave Cash time to herself, but he was beginning to feel as if he was failing her. In Kellz's eyes, he was sent to protect not only her heart but to mend the broken pieces and regain happiness. He was very understanding when it came to her situation, which was why he let her grieve in peace.

On many occasions Kellz caught Cash crying, but he would ignore her hurt to mask his own pain. It killed him to know he couldn't replace Nino because he had given all he had to give. He waited on Cash hand and foot. He made sure to step up to the plate of being a father. He made sure to put Cash's needs first, but it seemed as if it wasn't enough. He knew inside he made Cash happy, but she didn't have that same glow she had the first time he met her. Just like now, he watched her on the balcony, and she appeared out of it. Since the day of the movie, she had been distant and spent more time in her office. Cash hadn't mentioned the seminar to Kellz, so she was gonna find a way to escape without his knowledge.

"You hungry?" Kellz asked, knowing the answer. Just as he figured, Cash shook her head no. He let out a small sigh because the way she had been behaving was taking a toll on their relationship. "Look, ma. I know you don't wanna talk about it, but I'm getting fed up with your distance. Cash, yo' ass ain't ate, you barley sleep and you be zoning out on a nigga. I'm no fool. I saw exactly what you saw in that theater. I know the shit seems like something it may not be. It's just a movie. Let that shit go." Kellz watched her pensively.

"If it's bothering you that much, then maybe we need time apart from each other. You or no one else can tell me a movie was ironically shot with the same shit that happened to me. Did you see that woman? She looked just like me. Did you see the woman's mother? Oh, no, I'm not gonna believe for one second that it's just a movie. That motherfucker has made a carbon copy movie of my damn life!" Cash raised her voice in frustration.

"So what you wanna do? Sue?"

"Sue?" Cash questioned because a lawsuit just wasn't enough. "I'll take matters into my own hands." Cash turned away from Kellz and stepped back onto her balcony.

"So what the fuck you gon' do, Cash?" he asked, because he knew what it meant for Cash to take matters into her own hands. He knew exactly the measures Cash would go to when someone crossed her. At this point, he couldn't do anything but shake his head. "Yo' plate gon' be on the stove." Kellz walked out of the room disgruntled.

He ignored the statement about time apart because he knew she was talking out of emotions. It hurt him because he was trying to be there for her, but she continued to shut him out. However, if she kept it up, he would give her the *time apart* she requested.

***

"I'm telling you, Jackie, something just wasn't right."

"I watched it last night, and from what I've read, and you told me, Cash, you not tripping. There's someone making millions off your life. A life that ended drastically. The shit ain't cool because you lost too many loved ones, so you're not wrong about how you feel. I say let's kill him." Jackie spoke as if murder wasn't nothing. Jackie Snow was just as ruthless as Cash Lopez, and if it was anybody that Cash knew she could trust with her life, it was Jackie.

"So there's this seminar coming up in a few days. He's speaking and winning some sort of award." Cash handed Jackie the documents she had printed.

"So are you gonna go?" Jackie asked as she began reading over the pages.

"Hell yeah. I'm just trying to figure out what I'mma do about Kellz. He's been bugging over this. Nigga gon' try to say, 'Cash it's just a movie.' Just a movie my ass. Yeah, it's just a movie, but it's *my* fucking movie." Cash looked off pissed. The room fell silent for a brief moment until she realized Jackie was dealing with her own problems. "So how is he?" she asked, referring to Kango.

"He's okay. Hell, Kango in the M. She better get her mind right before he catches one of these big booty beach girls to occupy his time."

"That nigga in love. His ass ain't going nowhere. In here tearing down my damn doors."

They both shared a laugh.

Cash was pleasantly happy for Fin. The entire ideal of love wooed her in every time. It reminded her of the days she and Nino's love was desirable. Nino fought for every ounce of her love and even killed his baby mother to prove it. The son that Tiffany and Nino shared also died on the ship during the explosion. Although Cash wasn't fond of his mother, she took Braylen in as her own.

"She still won't speak to me," Jackie added with more sentiment. She loved Fin and wished she'd give her a chance to redeem herself. She didn't mean for things to pan out the way they did, and if she knew hurting Fin would be a part of history, she would have re-written her life.

"Just give her some time. She'll come around. They enrolled into school, so that's where they've been."

"What is she taking?"

"I'm not sure. She really doesn't talk much about it, but I've heard her mention an eyelash bar. Speaking of, your boy came in talking about a shop he's buying."

"Papi?"

"Yes, but guess who's shop it is?" Cash smirked, followed by an eye roll. "Girl, Monique," she added when she had Jackie's full attention.

"Liyah gonna kill that little nigga." Jackie rubbed her belly as she shook her head. "Speaking of the devil."

Papi walked into the room and all eyes shifted on him to him. The way he strolled in ruffled Jackie's feathers. She sat back in her seat and admired him with her eyes. He was wearing all-white, but she could tell he had the garments on the day before. It only turned her on more because it only showed he was a real trap boy.

"What's up with y'all hoochies?" Papi laughed, plopping down onto the sofa.

"Nigga, we ain't no hoochies. And where the hell have you been?"

"Trappin', ma. Jackie, what's up with yo' fine ass?" Papi flirted with the biggest smile. His smile was one of his biggest assets. Anytime he was in a room, he would steal every woman's attention with his pearly whites.

"Nothing, nigga. Get the fuck out and leave my friend alone, hoochie." Cash mugged Papi playfully.

"Ma, you know this my ole' lady. She need to stop playing wit' a nigga." Papi bit into his bottom lip while eyeing Jackie's breasts that sat up in her halter dress.

"Papi!" Cash yelled because she noticed the way he and Jackie were eye fucking one another.

"A'ight, damn. But look, though. I cashed ole girl out on the shop. Mama, I need you to run it. It can be the next Trap Girl."

"BJ, I'm not running that hoe shop."

"It's, Papi, girl," he defended to his mother. "Jackie, what's up? You new in town. You wanna run a—" Papi stopped mid-sentence when he noticed Liyah and Fin walking through the door. He still hadn't told Liyah about the shop because he knew she would trip. However, thanks to Cash, she asked the question without his approval.

"Liyah, you ready to run a shop?" Cash asked, being petty.

Liyah looked puzzled, but she shrugged her shoulders. "What shop? I don't know," she second guessed. Liyah didn't need a hair salon because she was covered in dough. It really wasn't her dream anyways. Liyah wanted to open a male exotic club but had never got around to it.

"Fin, you want to open your lash bar?" Cash asked because she noticed Fin trying to run for the back room.

Fin stopped midstride and turned on the heel of her shoes. She slightly rolled her eyes because she didn't want to be anywhere around Jackie. "Sure." Fin shrugged just as Liyah had done, but she was more interested.

"Yeah, lil' sis, you can run it," Papi added because he wanted no parts of Liyah being anywhere near a business Monique once owned.

"I'll fix it up for you," Jackie added, and the entire room fell silent.

"I don't need anything for you. Plus, I have the money," Fin retorted.

"And where did you get the money?" Cash asked because she saw a cat fight ready to transpire right in her living room.

Jackie remained quiet out of guilt. Had this been anyone else, she would have exploded.

"Financial aid," Liyah quickly replied. "So where is it?" she then asked, and Papi, Cash and Jackie looked at one another from the corner of their eyes.

"I bought the bitch, Monique, old shop. Hoe couldn't afford it, so it was being auctioned off," Cash replied, covering for her son.

"You could, Mommy." Liyah burst into laughter.

Papi scratched his head and let out a sigh.

Suddenly, Kellz emerged from nowhere, so the room's attention now shifted to him. He and Cash hadn't spoken all day, so she only watched him as he made his way to the door. Cash so badly wanted to call out to him, but she knew he would reject her. The statement she made about time apart reigned heavy on her mind as she tried to sleep through the night. She didn't mean to hurt nor offend him, but she needed to deal with the situation with a clear head.

"Well, I'll take you by there later so you can check it out," Papi told Fin, then headed down the hall in search of his son.

Liyah watched him closely through the slit of her eyes. She was upset he didn't come home last night but because there was a room full of people, she let it ride. She knew his excuse would be the club because it closed at 5 AM. He would always mention staying over a few hours after, which meant he'd miss Liyah because she left early for school.

Everyone began to chat, and the entire time, Cash noticed Jackie sneaking peeks at Fin. She could tell Jackie was hurt by Fin's choice of words, but just as she told Jackie, Fin needed time to come around. At this very moment, she couldn't concentrate on Fin and Jackie because she had bigger issues ahead. She was ready for her trip to the Gulf of Mexico, and once she found out the information she needed, she could focus on her family, and soon to be husband.

CHAPTER 11

KANGO

"If I call you bae, you bae for the day
Or a bae for the night, you not my wife
She want a killer to fuck all night
I wanna fuck on a thot, gimmie head all night..."
- Pop Smoke

Opening his eyes at the crack of dawn, Kango hopped out of his king-sized bed ready for his day. He headed into the restroom and began running his shower. He pulled his toothbrush from the holder and began handling his hygiene. He then climbed into the shower and let the hot water wake up his game. He began soaping up then rinsed off. When he stepped out the shower, he wrapped into his towel, then headed into his bedroom to dress. He pressed play on his music, which was something he did every morning. Kango, his aunt and Jackie's crib was already plush with furniture, so he had everything in his bedroom to entertain himself.

Playing his music was something he always did when he moved around his room. At this moment, his choice of artist was Pop Smoke because he needed to stay grounded with his thoughts. This was his last straw with Fin, although he was already doing him. Yesterday, he spent the last of his Miami night cuddled up in VIP with a new jump-off. Tonight, he was hitting Papi's club, and he knew there would be mad bitches flocking. However, his heart yearned for, Fin so he wasn't giving up that easy. He was giving her the time she asked for, but he'd be damned if he let her go completely.

Once Kango was done, he headed through the newly reno-vated home and strolled to his whip. He made sure to stop into his aunt's room to let her know he would return later. He hit the alarm on his AMG and climbed in. He immediately powered on his radio and connected his Bluetooth from his cell phone. After choosing the proper song, Kango pulled off to his destination. He was to arrive at 7:19 AM. He pushed the pedal to the metal, and the entire way, he prepared a speech in hopes to get his girl back.

When Kango arrived at Dade University, he jumped out of his ride and headed for the office. He walked into the office with confidence and approached the counter to give them Enfinity's real name. The receptionist that handled administration began to punch Fin's name in the computer. She searched three differ-ent databases until she found her.

"Okay, sir, her classroom is building D 429. Do you have an ID?"

"Yes, ma'am." Kango reached into his pocket. The en-tire time, the administrator eyed him, seductively wishing he would make small talk. However, Kango remained quiet be-cause he was here for one thing and one thing only.

After retrieving his ID, Kango headed through campus in search of building D. Everyone watched him in awe wondering if he had enrolled. The women chanted and the guys whispered, but he kept right on his mission. Once he finally found the class-room, Kango stuck his head inside. His eyes scanned the entire room, but there was no sign of Enfinity. He shook his head, tired of looking like a fool, so he headed back for his car. The moment he fell into his seats, he pulled out his cell and dialed her num-ber.

"Hello?"

"Where the fuck you at, Fin?"

"I'm at school."

He could hear the nervousness in her voice. "No the fuck you ain't because I'm at your school." Kango was pressured.

"You're at my school?" Fin asked nervously as if she hadn't heard a word.

"A'ight you wanna keep playing wit' a nigga? Yeah, a'ight."

"Kango, I'm not...I'm not playing with you."

"Man, fuck you." Kango pressed the end button on his phone and dropped it inside of the center console. He turned his music up to the max and headed for the highway to meet Jackie. On his way, he hadn't heard his phone constantly ringing, and he didn't bother to look at it. He knew Fin would try to reach out but he was done; or, at least he kept telling himself that. It was time to focus on his bag and push Fin far back in his mind. He was tired of the kid games. He understood her reasons for being upset, but she continued to shut him out while he tried hard to shower her with love. He knew Fin would come running back; hopefully it wouldn't be too late.

***

"She know I'm nasty (yeah)
She like when I pull it out and I put it all
over her ass cheeks (like, uh, ooh)
And she don't gotta ask me (come on)
Yeah, I want head before we fuck and I want it nasty..."

Kango bit into his bottom lip as he watched a stallion by the name of Mahogany slide two of her fingers inside of her pussy. When she pulled them out, she stuck them into her mouth and sucked off her own juices as if she was sucking Kangos dick. Mahogany was intrigued by Kango's whole style of fashion, and she could tell he was holding. She silently prayed inside she was doing a number on him in hopes to be the lucky chick of the night. She wanted Kango in the worst way—just as she wanted Papi once upon a time. She couldn't front, his entire crew had swagger, and because they were all posted in VIP with the owner, she knew they were well connected. After Papi had pretty much shitted on her, she decided to go for the next best thing.

Kango took notice of how territorial Mahogany was acting, but because of her beauty, he didn't mind. She was a redbone with a long weave and exotic eyes. The oversized butterfly tattoo on her ass turned him on, along with the nipple piercings that also had butterfly rings. Truthfully, all the women in Papi's club were bombshells, and they were handpicked by Papi himself.

"Ayo, you wild, ma." Goon pulled Kango's attention. He smacked the chick that was dancing on him on the ass, then pulled her down into his lap.

Kango laughed because Goon was having the time of his life. Tonight was his second time meeting Goon, and he liked his style. Goon was young, wild but got to the money before the worms surfaced from their hiding places.

"Come do that trick again." Kango looked at Mahogany.

She knew exactly what trick he referred to, and she was pleased he asked. She took the champagne bottle and laid down on the black velvet sofa. She inserted the bottle into her opening and began to flex her muscles. Kango pulled the bottle out of her pussy, and she began to massage her clit. He smiled. *1, 2, 3...* he counted in his head, and just as he got to 3, champagne began squirting from inside of her.

"Yo', you a fucking savage." He smiled widely showing his beautiful white teeth. He began throwing stacks of money at her, and she deserved every dollar. "Come here." He pulled her down onto his lap and didn't care if champagne got on his pants. His dick was hard, and he wanted so bad to get some head right there in VIP. However, Kango had morals and more respect for women.

"You leaving with me tonight?"

"Yeah...I mean if you want me too."

"Unless you got something to do."

"Yeah, *you.*" She smirked seductively. Inside, she was screaming, *hell yes,* but she couldn't look like a groupie. Out of all the men she danced for, it was something about Kango she took a liking too. After they fucked, she wanted more than just a one night stand. She wasn't trying to be his girl or anything, but she wanted to kick with him on more than one occasion. The only problem was, she was hoping Papi hadn't smutted her name.

CHAPTER 12

ENFINITY

"No more empty conversation
Next time I will be totally sure
Don't want the pain of falling
In and out of love..."
- Brandy

"He isn't answering my calls. I guess it's really over."

"I told you to give him a chance. Trust me, Miami is the last place you want him to wander off into. All these thirsty hoes out here would love to snag a man like Kango."

"Well, if he can't wait for me, then we don't need to be together."

"I'm sure he can wait for you, but knowing how men are, he's probably doing him in the meantime."

"They can have him." Fin tried hard to convince herself. If Kango left her, she would die. She had already died a thousand times since the day they last spoke. And now that he wasn't answering her calls, she was mortified.

"Well, let's go out. Go to your room and slide into something sexy. Lord knows I need a good outing and a drink." Liyah began moving around her room. She walked to her closet to find an outfit, and when her eyes fell on the Alexander McQueen dress she had been dying to wear, she pulled it off the hanger.

Hearing that they were going out was music to Fin's ears. She jumped to her feet and rushed into her room to do the same. She anxiously browsed through her closet and picked up a sexy bodycon dress made by Rasario. Liyah didn't have to tell her twice. She pinned up her hair and began to run her shower. This would be her first time going out since her transition to Miami. She hoped they ended up in Papi's club so Papi could tell Kango how sexy she looked and how loose she was behaving. Tonight she was gonna let her hair down, and if God allowed, she was gonna meet her a friend or two. Fin was tired of being Miss Goody Two-Shoes. And what Liyah said about Kango being entertained by women only gave her more confidence to move on.

After Fin's showered, she oiled down in her coco body oil and sprayed her best perfume. It was Paris Hilton, which was Kango's favorite. She slid into her dress and found the perfect heels to match. Once she was done, she grabbed her diamond clutch and headed into Liyah's bedroom. When she walked in, Liyah was wrapped in a towel fresh out of the shower. She was patting Escolan's back, and he was nearly asleep.

Fin tiptoed through the room so she didn't wake the baby. She went into the restroom to touch up her hair and makeup. She applied the twenty-four hour edge control to her baby hairs and let her pins out. She then applied a small dose of lip gloss with eyeliner. Her Dubi lashes had just been done two days previous, and that's all it took to bring out the diva within. She couldn't wait until she opened her lash bar and could rock her own product. Papi was supposed to take her to the shop to check it out, but, of course, he got consumed with work. After a little snooping, Fin found out it was Papi who actually bought it, but it wasn't her business, so she hadn't mentioned it to Liyah.

What Papi didn't know was, Fin had the money to cash him out, so she was gonna put up an offer. After all the meth she and Liyah had been selling, she had well over a hundred grand saved from profit alone. They still had nearly three hundred grand in work that she knew would sell quickly. The once timid girl had blossomed into a real Trap Princess, and because of how easy the money was coming in, she was becoming addicted to her new hustle. She was finally able to provide for herself and live out her boss dreams.

Her and Liyah were going to the dealership next week because Fin wanted to cop a new ride. Liyah had plenty of high in vehicles, but she mentioned being bored with them. Therefore, she was gonna get something new, and she had her heart set on a baby pink Bugatti truck.

After Fin was done, Escolan was fast asleep, so Liyah began sliding into her dress. Her hair was already intact, so Fin knew they would be leaving shortly.

"So where we going?" Fin asked in a whisper.

"To Papi's." Liyah smirked because she too wanted to show up and show out.

"Good," Fin replied, and matched her smirk. This was perfect for her plan, but little did she know, Kango was already in attendance, and he wasn't alone.

***

When Liyah and Fin pulled up to the club, the line was still wrapped around the corner. Tonight, they decided to take a driver so they could get drunk as ever and enjoy their outing. The driver pulled the Rolls Royce Cullinan to the front entrance and climbed out to open the doors. When the two stepped out, the chatter amongst the party goers were commended. Everyone knew Liyah, and they also knew she was the first lady. The way she looked and stepped out of the car with confidence only added to her assertiveness. Every woman wanted to be in her shoes, and every man wanted a piece of her. However, everyone knew the extent of where the fearless Papi Carter would go if he was crossed. The city feared Papi, so the many lusts would be kept to a minimum.

"Hey, Boss Lady." The guard at the front door lifted the

rope to escort them inside. When they walked further into the club, they were greeted by the host that collected the money.

"Hey, Liy Liy. I'll send your bottles up."

"Thank you, Tiana." Liyah smiled and pulled Fin by the arm.

"I don't wanna go to the VIP yet, but there's a small VIP on the dance floor, so we can turn up for a minute there."

"I'm with it." Fin was game.

They made their way through the small crowd to the VIP on the first floor. Liyah wanted Fin to enjoy herself, so she decided against the VIP that was upstairs. Not to mention she knew Papi was probably up there, and she didn't want to ruin their fun so soon.

Once inside the small section, the guards posted up nearby the moment their eyes fell onto their boss lady. Liyah whispered to David, the head of security, and told him to radio in two double shots of XO to start them off for the night. After a five minute wait, their drinks had arrived, and they began drinking eagerly. Tonight, Fin put her big girl panties on because she wanted to loosen up.

"That's my shit!" Fin shouted to Liyah as the beat dropped to Megan Thee Stallion's "Freak Nasty." They both began to dance right there where they stood because the dance floor was extremely crowded. Everyone danced, had fun and this was the part Liyah hated. She couldn't enjoy herself like the rest of the patrons because she still had to be on point. Although she had guards surrounding her, that didn't excuse the Ruger SR40 in her purse. Liyah wasn't a basic bitch, and she knew that in the blink of an eye, a small time hustler would try her. After everything she'd been through in her life, she didn't trust a soul. Therefore, as the great Cash Lopez imprinted in her, shoot first and ask questions never.

"There go, Papi." Liyah nudged Fin's shoulder. They both looked upstairs into the VIP, and after heavily studying Papi's circle, Kango came into view.

"Damn, Kango here." Fin's heart began to race, and when

she saw him being entertained by some chick, the rate of her heartbeat sped up and began pumping with anger.

"Let's go up there." Liyah swallowed the last bit of her glass.

The fun Fin wanted to have was out of the window because things had just heated up. She was gonna ignore him and maybe do a little flirting herself. She did the same as Liyah and swallowed the rest of her drink. They headed out of the VIP followed by two guards that stood at least six-seven. The girls were led upstairs, ready to make their surprise entrance. Little did Liyah know, Papi was in the clear because he was already informed of her presence. Kango, on the other hand, was unaware because Papi didn't get a chance to tell him. By the time Papi made his way over, the girls were already coming up the stairs. When Kango noticed Fin, he wanted so bad to jump out of his seat, but a more petty plan had crossed his mind.

Fin walked into the VIP and stood behind Liyah ignoring Kango. Kango sat with Mahogany, who was now dressed and anxiously waited for them to leave. Kango didn't flex a muscle because he was gonna play her game with her. However, his eyes wandered up and down her body, and the dress she wore was too provocative. He had to laugh to keep from getting upset. He continued to watch her through the dark shades that hovered his eyes, but no one took notice.

"What's up, baby daddy?" Liyah leaned over to utter into Papi's ear.

"What's up, wife." He matched her energy, then pulled her into his chest. "I see your little section over there set up. Now take yo' ass over there and behave, Liy Liy. You and Fin bet not start no shit up in here tonight, and on my daddy grave, not one nigga bet not even look y'all way." Papi held his composure trying hard not to flip out. Liyah wasn't looking like the normal mommy from back at home. Instead, she was looking like a single, sexy, rich slut.

"Yes, daddy." She smirked and kissed him on the lips. Papi bit into her bottom lip, then released her with a slap on the ass."

"What's up, Kango?" Liyah fetched before walking off to their section.

"Sup, sis." Kango nodded his head but ignored Fin.

Fin's palms were sweaty, but she tried hard to keep her composure.

"Hiii, Liyah." Mahogany smiled hard, happy to be within three feet from Liyah.

Liyah looked at her and only flashed a fake smile. She spent on the heel of her six-inch stilettos and pulled Fin to their VIP. Fin began dancing trying her best to act unfazed. Liyah began to pour them a glass because she sensed Fin's infuriation.

"Don't sweat that childish shit, Fin. Trust me, that hoe ain't nobody." Liyah mugged Mahogany. She didn't care how nice the bitches in the club pretended to be; she didn't trust them. They all were in love with Papi, and she knew he'd probably smashed half of them.

"I'm not sweating him, Liyah. Maybe it's time we move on. Speaking of, who's that?" Fin pointed to Goon, who sat on the other side of Papi.

"Girl, that's Papi boy. And I know yo' ass ain't thinking about?"

"He's coming over. Oh my God," Fin whispered nervously.

"Sup, Liy Liy?" Goon walked into the VIP with a motive.

Fin looked him up and down impressed. Goon was fine as hell and the total opposite of Kango. He had a pair of broad shoulders with huge arms. His Falcons fitted hat sat on top of his head, but his deep jet black waves peeked through the hole. His huge diamond earrings shined bright, but not as bright as his smile with a pair of deep dimples.

"Hey, Goon," Liyah replied, noticing how Goon was eyeing Fin. "This is Enfinity." Liyah introduced.

"What's up, Enfinity? Goon," he introduced himself.

"Nice to meet you." Fin blushed.

From across the room, Kango watched the extreme smile on Fin's face, angry. He knew Goon was just being a man and because he never mentioned Fin being his girl, she was actually fair game. He didn't wanna look like a hater, so he remained seated.

"Where you get her from, Liy Liy? How come I ain't never saw her sexy ass?"

"She's from Cali, and, nigga, she's spoken for," Liyah replied, because she saw the way Kango was watching them.

Fin had also taken notice, so she invited Goon to have a seat beside her.

"You're playing with fire." Liyah Leaned over to whisper in her ear.

"It's called fighting fire with fire." Fin felt like she was on the winning end.

Her and Goon began to talk, and after almost thirty minutes, Kango couldn't stand the sight of her. He stood to his feet, and Fin was smiling on the sly. She thought Kango was on his way over but, he fooled the hell out of them. He helped Mahogany to her feet and dapped Papi. Papi began to smile while shaking his head, and now Kango had the winning lead. He walked out of the VIP with his lady friend close behind. They made their way down the stairs, and with each step Fin's heart sank more.

Not being able to control her emotions, she jumped to her feet and stormed down the steps two at a time. She didn't wanna disrespect Papi's club, but she'd be damned if Kango disrespected her. When she made it outdoors, Kango had just opened the door for Mahogany and let her climb into his passenger seat. Just as he closed the door, Fin's fragrance brought him to a halt. Feeling the effects of the liquor, Fin rushed the passenger door and tugged at the handle. When she realized it was locked, she began banging on the window. Kango quickly rushed back over when he noticed Mahogany trying to get out. Mahogany was a street chick; don't let the prettiness fool ya. However, knowing she had come with Liyah, she was a bit scared. She had seen Liyah scarp and wanted no parts. Not only that, but she was Cash's daughter, and Mahogany dared to cross Cash Lopez.

"Man, watch out, Fin. You ain't about to touch this girl," Kango defended Mahogany. It wasn't so much as Mahogany he was concerned about. He was protecting her from what every-thing could escalate to.

"So you're taking up for the bitch?! Nigga, you got me fucked up if you think you 'bout to leave with this two dolla, hoe!"

"Look, Fin, you ain't my bitch, yo'! Get the fuck on, ma. And on God, if you touch my whip, I'mma break yo' fucking face!" Kango spewed.

Fin's chest heaved up and down, but the way his voice blared, she knew he wasn't playing. She looked at him with so much embarrassment and pain. Kango wanted badly to end the fury, but all he could think about was the way Fin was playing with him. He looked her in the eyes, and a part of him knew he was making a mistake, but he couldn't break. He walked off leaving Fin standing outside alone. She watched the car as it pulled off praying he would come to his senses. When the car turned at the light, Fin knew right then she lost him for good. Tears began to pour from her eyes, and she suddenly felt dizzy. The thought of Kango fucking Mahogany only added to her de-ception. She couldn't believe he would go this far to hurt her. She turned to walk back into the club, and a perfectly good night was now ruined.

CHAPTER 13

CASH LOPEZ

"You're everything I need and more
It's written all over your face
Baby, I can feel your halo
Pray it won't fade away..."
- Beyoncé

"**A**nd for the moment you all have been waiting for. This man is unbelievable, and I'm honored to have worked with him. Some would consider him a simple doctor, but our community considers him a hero. Everyone, please stand to your feet and give a round of applause for Doctor David Stine."

The entire conference stood to their feet and began clapping as if the President of the United States had taken the stage. There were at least 2,000 people in attendance to pay homage to the doctor everyone had known as Doctor Stine.

Cash Lopez stood in the far back dressed in a pair of scrubs and lab coat to blend in with the entire room. She watched astounded as everyone praised the man as if he was some sort of Doctor God. The room was in an uproar, and it only made her wonder what more was he being awarded for. She continued to watch as a lady walked up and placed a huge trophy on the podium.

Doctor Stine looked around the room proud of himself. He had accomplished something no human being could accomplish. It would take a lifetime of college courses to fill the doctor's shoes. And this was why he was referred to as the Einstein of Doctors. Every hospital around the world paid top dollar for Doctor Stine to fly in and perform surgeries that only a man in his stature could perform. He was ruled king, and Cash had gotten her chance to see it up close and personal.

"Sir, how's Abdullah doing?" one doctor asked, making everyone laugh.

"He's 100 percent, Doc. Thanks for asking."

Abdullah?

Cash wondered who was the person everyone spoke upon. The doctor had been bombarded with questions about this Abdullah Hassan character that was being described as some sort of science project.

"Doctor Stine, how's the book coming along?" another nurse asked, and this brought Cash to a standstill.

She watched the gleam in his eyes at the mention of his book. Again, he smiled proudly, then began discussing content inside. After several more questions, Cash learned this book was a life story based around Abdullah Hassan, just as the movie. Cash thought of Kellz words *It's just a movie* and wondered if she was overreacting.

The conference went on for another hour, and the entire time, Doctor Stine had the floor. Cash wanted so badly to leave, but she was in deliberation with herself. She just couldn't leave without speaking with Doctor Stine. Therefore, she waited until the conference was over and discreetly followed him to his vehicle. She climbed into her car and watched as he climbed into his 2020 Chevy Silverado. As Doctor Stine removed his coat, Cash used this time to slide into her all black tee and tights. She threw on her black hooded sweatshirt and covered her eyes with a pair of Marc Jacob box-frame shades.

When he pulled out of the huge lot, Cash gave him some time before she trailed behind. She made sure to keep a nice gap in between so he wouldn't notice he was being followed. Doctor Stine jumped on the freeway, and Cash noticed the sign that read Guanajuato. The drive was about another thirty minutes out, which was a total of an hour and fifteen minutes from the stadium. Cash made sure to store the information in her memory bank so she could keep track of her locations.

After the thirty minute ride, Doctor Stine exited the highway, and Cash recited the sign that read De Allende. It was a small road that led to extremely large homes in the middle of nowhere.

"Thirteen minutes."

Cash looked down at her watch assuming this was the doctors home that sat at the end of the road. She stopped on her breaks and pulled alongside a house as if she was a residence. From where she parked, she could hear the sound of Doctor Stine's truck sliding across the dirt field yard. She also heard the sound of a dog barking in the distance, and she knew the dog belonged to Stine. Because he had turned his headlights off, she couldn't see what took place in the yard. Once she heard his car door slam, she gave him about twenty minutes before she made her move towards the home.

She pulled out of the yard and pulled further into the woods to camouflage her vehicle. Cash then reached into her bag, pulled out her 9 millimeter and tucked it into her pants. Before stepping out of the car, she let out a timorous sigh, then looked over to the home.

"Here we go." She stepped out and crept like a thief in the night. She made sure to pull her hoodie back so she didn't alarm the dog. "Come here, boy." Cash spoke in an even tone making sure not to startle her.

Kona quickly turned around to the sound of Cash's voice, but she didn't bother to bark. Normally, Kona would bark because anyone who wasn't Abdullah, Doctor, or Charlotte was considered an intruder.

"Mwah, mwah, mwah." Cash kissed the dog over as she patted her knees.

Kona began walking in the direction of the estranged woman. Cash let out a sigh and began rubbing underneath her chin for comfort. When she had her where she wanted, she got up and headed for the home. The exterior of the home was one hundred sixteen acres, but this meant nothing to a woman like Cash Lopez. She turned on her prowler instincts, and within seconds, she was inside the home.

"Hello, Doctor Stine." Cash held her gun pointed at the doctor, who had just emerged from the kitchen. The glass that contained a cup of grapefruit justice crashed into the floor.

"What the...!" Doctor was startled. His heart began to pump with fear as he stared into the eyes of Cash Lopez.

Inside of the bedroom, Abdullah heard the glass crash into the floor, followed by the shaken sound in Doctor Stine's voice. This alerted him, and his hood instincts immediately kicked in. He grabbed his strap from the dresser and jumped to his feet. He made his way slowly down the hall until he reached the front room. From where he stood, Doctor Stine could see him, but the intruder couldn't. He looked into the doctor's eyes, and there was something about the way he looked. His fear quickly changed to worry, and this made Abdullah wonder what was so impelling. He raised his gun and took another step into the open room. When he came face to face with the person dressed in a hoodie, his initial reaction was to shoot. However, the world stopped, and the pulsation of his heart began to thump rapidly.

Cash quickly turned her gun towards the man that had appeared from the dark hallway and she too stopped because it was as if she had seen a ghost.

"Nino?" Cash apprehensively spoke his name. She lowered her gun and her head fell to the side. A mournful gush of fluid raced through her body, and she felt as if she would pass out. They watched each other as if they both were in an alluring dream until tears welled up in all four pairs of eyes. *This can't be*, Cash thought as her hands began to neurotically shake. Her body became weak, and she suddenly dropped to her knees. "Ninooooo…" She began to sob, and a waterfall of tears began to pour from her eyes.

  This couldn't be the man she longed for. The man she would give her own life to bring back. The man she spent countless years crying for. He was here in the flesh, and they'd encountered each other after nearly twenty years of living the nightmare of being apart. It was him; Brooklyn Nino.

CHAPTER 14

KELLZ

"It feels like I've just walked right out of heaven,
It feels like I've damn near thrown my life away
I'm scared just like a child that's lost at seven
Don't know what to do, to get back right with you..."
- Jagged Edge

(Previously In Cash Lopez)

A nigga couldn't be more happier with life. I finally got to be with my kids, because they bitter ass momma finally accepted the fact that we were done. At times, I felt like I was making a bad decision, but everyday Cash proved me wrong. We were thick as thieves, except for the one trip every month she took to her punk ass baby daddy house. I swear if I ever found out she was giving that nigga my pussy, I'mma bury both they ass in Forest Lawn Cemetery. I sacrificed so much to be with Cash so I'd be damned if she played a nigga.

The night she had the run in with Que, a nigga was worried shitless. I was blowing up her phone but never got an answer. A part of me thought her ass was somewhere getting ratchet, but the other part of me knew that wasn't the case. If it was one thing I knew about Cash, was, her ass was gonna handle her business first and she wasn't gonna stop until the shit was handled.

Imagine my surprise when I got a call from MPD to pick her up. I would go into details but I'mma let her tell y'all that part. I fully turned over the restaurant's back to Cash and Papi and was now focusing on my laundromats. I was in the process of opening up a

*movie theater called Brooklyn Cinema and I couldn't wait. Despite me
fucking with Cash, I missed the fuck out my dog. I always thought
back to our conversation and laughed every time.*

*"Something ever happen to a nigga, I need you to be there for
my girl."*

"What you mean nigga?"

*"Like be there for her. I'm not saying marry her or nothing, but
shit if you gotta marry her, do it. I don't want no new nigga around
my seed Kellz."*

*"Ha ha ha, man you crazy as hell nigga. So you telling me you
want me to wife your wife?"*

*"Shit if that's how you put it. I don't trust nobody with her, or
my businesses."*

"I feel you but nigga that's crazy."

We both laughed.

*I wanted to tell Cash about that conversation so bad, but I
didn't want her tripping. I knew Cash like a book, and her ass would
probably dig Nino up just to kick his ass then bury him again, so I left
it alone. On another note, It's crazy how in one year, Cash made me
happier than my wife of 16 years. I loved the ground that girl walked
on, and I wouldn't trade her for the world. Couldn't no bitch in the
state of Florida fuck with Cash and that's how it's been, and would always be.*

T ossing and turning in his king sized bed, Kellz couldn't
sleep without Cash wrapped in his arms. For several
days, he'd been dealing with sleepless nights, but tonight
was worse. It was now four in the morning, and Cash hadn't so
much as called. Thoughts of her being harmed crossed his mind,
but he knew better. Cash was up to something she had no business, and he felt it in the mere pit of his stomach. The moment
she walked into their home he was gonna let her have it. After-
wards, it was time they put the fire out that had been brewing

between them.

It had been a few days since the slick ass comment she made about *time apart*. Since he hadn't spoken to her because he was giving her the space she requested, he expected her to at least apologize. But not once did she repair the damage she had caused. Being hurt would be an understatement; Kellz felt betrayed because she was choosing an illusion over his heart. He saw exactly what she had seen on that screen, but just as he told her, she was tripping. Another part of him tugged at his mind, and knowing Cash Lopez, she was on a hunt for the person responsible. This was the one thing about her he hated.

She would always count him out of her minacious lifestyle. He'd told her on many occasions to let him be the man, but Cash just had to wear the pants. He remembered when she was with Nino she was the same way. At this point, he felt foolish for thinking he could change her ways. Over the course of time, Cash did change, and he had to give her, that but what bothered him most was the drug selling and senseless killings. Between the dough Kellz was packing and what Cash brought to the table, the two were beyond rich. Even Papi could get out the game and they would be straight. They all had successful businesses that made tons of money, and their grandkids would be straight.

Feeling defeated, Kellz rolled over and picked up his phone from the dresser. His pride wouldn't let him call for days in, but tonight, he had to swallow the macho man attitude and see where his woman was located. He dialed Cash's number, and it went to voicemail on the first ring. He dialed her for a second time to make sure he wasn't tripping, and the same thing happened. Shaking his head Kellz, placed his phone back down.

"Kelly, I can't sleep." Skylar barged into the room in a frantic.

"You good, lil' baby? You had a nightmare?"

"Yes. I had a bad dream. Where's Mommy?"

"Mommy not here right now. You can lay down right here."

Kellz lifted from the bed and let Skylar climb in. He went and took a seat on the chase and powered on the television. He watched Skylar as she snuggled into Cash's pillow. He knew she had done this because it had her mother's scent. Within minutes, Skylar was sound asleep, but he didn't take her into her room. He chose to stay seated on the chase, and he was gonna wait for Cash to walk through the door with an explanation.

From time to time, Kellz would look over to Skylar, and it made him miss his daughters. Since he'd been with Cash, he hadn't spent much time with them because he wasn't under the same roof. The last two days he had stopped by, but it was something strange about the way his ex-wife had been acting. She was getting used to his visits and would be all in his face. He didn't want her to have the wrong impression, so he would simply leave. Earlier this evening, she had sent him a text that read *Wyd*. He was surprised because she hadn't shown any concern since he left her for Cash. Just thinking about his family, that he pretty much abandoned, made him feel guilty. He picked up the phone and did something that even shocked him. He texted Adrina.

4:29 AM *Kellz: You sleep?*

Kellz sat his phone in his lap. He looked back at the television and tried hard to focus on Martin roasting Pam. His phone began to ring, and he quickly looked down in hopes that it was Cash. Instead, it was Adrina.

"Sup?"

"Kelly? Are you okay?" she asked worried.

"Yeah, I'm straight. Just up watching Martin."

"Oh, okay. Where's Cash?" Drina asked, knowing she couldn't possibly be anywhere around. Kellz wouldn't dare talk to her in front of Cash. Whenever he called, it was always simply about his children.

"She's out of town doing some shit for the club."

"Oh, okay." There was a slight pause, and Drina could hear

Martin playing in the background. "Are you okay?" she asked, because she sensed something wasn't right.

"I'm good. Why you say that?"

"Because I was with you since high school. Kelly, I know you like a book. Now talk to me because you know I'm here if you need me."

"I know." Kellz nodded his head. He couldn't take that from Drina no matter what. Although he got bored with her and found excitement in dating Cash, there were still small sentimental things he remembered about the woman that once carried his last name. She would always show concern whenever Kellz was being put under the pressure of the streets. Not once did she judge his choice of hustle. She also stood by his side when he ran Nino's restaurant. "Nah, I'm good. So what you doing up, though?"

"Well, if you must know, I was pleasing myself."

"Pleasing yourself as in..."

"Yes." Drina giggled and made Kellz laugh along. "Hell, I can't remember the last time I got laid. Therefore, I take myself to ecstasy." Again, she laughed.

This surprised Kellz because that was another reason he started his affair with Cash. Drina was a boring fuck. There was no excitement, but what caught his attention was the fact that she mentioned she hadn't had sex. "Come on, ma. You ain't gotta lie to me. Somebody's been hitting that."

"I'm being honest. I mean, you got a girl, so why would I lie? I haven't had sex since the last time you hit it," she defended, embarrassed.

"So what size is it?" Kellz asked, curiously knowing he had no business.

"You wanna see it?"

"Sure," he replied, and a Facetime came through. When he answered, Drina was holding a nine-inch chocolate dildo. She waved it into the camera with a huge grin. Kellz laughed as his eyes fell down to the small red robe she was wearing, and he could tell she was naked underneath. Her bare nipple peaked out every now and then, and for some reason, Kellz was turned on.

Drina knowing Kellz saw the sudden change in his face and knew what it was all about. He was eyeing her body with hunger, so she took it upon herself to tease him. Drina knew she would never get a chance to have sex with Kellz again, but it would for sure turn her on if she could catch a cyber nut. She laid back on the bed with the phone in the air. Kellz sat back in his seat wondering what she was about to do. When she cocked her legs back, Kellz tuned further in. Drina then began to use the dildo to rub against her clit.

"Hold that thought real quick." Kellz quickly sat the phone down and headed over to the bed. He picked Skylar up and carried her next door to her bedroom. He powered on her night light, then quietly left back to his bedroom. When he picked the phone up, Drina had the dildo inserted inside of her, pulling it in and out. Kellz laid back on his bed. He watched Drina with an enthralling gaze.

"Bend over and insert it," he instructed, then pulled his dick from the top of his sweats. Kellz began stroking himself, but he didn't take his eyes from his phone. When Drina bent over, she tooted her ass in the air and inserted the dildo from behind. This really turned him on.

Kellz was in for a night of his life with someone he would least expect. For the next hour, he had totally forgotten about Cash, and it was going on nearly 6AM. After the fat nut he was gonna bust, he would finally get some sleep.

***

A Few Hours Later...

Kellz watched Cash on their home monitor as she sluggishly made her way down the driveway and to the front porch. He contemplated with himself if he wanted to ignore her, but he just couldn't, so he lifted from his seat so he could meet her at the front door. Just as he took the last step down, she came through the door wearing a sheepish look. It was like she could feel his presence because she quickly looked in his direction. Their eyes met, and it was something about her face that looked odd. Kellz could tell that she had been crying because her face was rosy red, and her eyes were puffy.

"Fuck you been, Cash?"

"Kellz..." Cash let out a deep sigh. She looked Kelly into his eyes apprehensively. The entire way home she contemplated on telling him her discoverance of Nino, but she knew it would tear them apart.

"I had to fly out to meet with this new connect. I'm plugging them with Jackie," Cash lied with a straight face.

"So why you been crying?"

"Crying?" Cash tried to mask her pain. "Oh, my allergies." She quickly thought of a lie.

Kellz knew better than to believe it, but he couldn't argue because Cash did have bad allergies. When she noticed he wouldn't say anything else, she used this as her chance to dodge him. She lied about going to find allergy medicine, so Kellz watched her dismiss herself. All he could do was shake his head because he saw their relationship going nowhere. He prayed by the end of the week Cash would realize she was destroying him and repair the love that existed just a week ago.

CHAPTER 15

BROOKLYN NINO

"Are we living a lie, baby
Is that magic gone
do you feel the same way you used to, girl
tell me is it wrong for us to love like this
How deep is your love?..."
-Keith Sweat

1 Month Later...

Brooklyn Nino sat in the window of the home he shared with Doctor Stine. The sky was gloomy as the grey clouds hovered over the home. The sound of thunder roared through the sky as the unyielding rain crashed into the mud. In the distance, Nino could see the headlights of a vehicle, and his heart began to beat attentively. When the car pulled into the yard, he watched it with ease until the headlights cut off and the engine went dead.

Cash Lopez jumped out of the car and pulled her hood over her head to keep from getting wet. It tripped Nino out how Kona never barked and would always run to Cash's side in protection. It made him think back to when he first met her and her aura alone attracted him.

"Hey."

Nino turned around to the sound of Cash's voice, and that same heartbeat from a month ago when they encountered each other after all this time had raced the same. Since that day, Cash had been creeping out to Guanajuato every chance she got.

"Sup, lil' mama." Nino flourished calling Cash by her old nickname.

Cash blushed and walked over to give him a hug. Nino wrapped his arms around her waist and kissed into her neck. The smell of her fragrance was alluring, and it made him never wanna let go. For an entire month, Cash had been wrapped in Nino's arms as if they were rekindling their marriage. Nino mentioned going back home with Cash on several occasions, however, Cash would always tell him the time wasn't right. They talked about everything since the explosion, but she failed to mention her relationship with Kellz, his son BJ still being alive and her child she bore with Braxton.

Cash did mention Breelah being alive, and she promised to bring her by soon. She also told him the jaw dropping story about Que's deception and Aaliyah killing her own father. Everything to Cash was so overwhelming. She just couldn't find a way to make her family work under the circumstances. Right now, she thought it was best Nino remained Abdullah, and when she found a way, she would bring him forward. For many nights, it hurt her soul to know she would have to hurt Kellz. She wished she could have her cake and eat it too, but after everything she experienced with Nino and Que, she thought against it. Lately, Kellz had been gone more, and Cash knew it was because he wanted attention. But it was perfect for Cash because it allowed her the time to run into the arms of the man that held her heart in the palm of his hands.

"You missed me?" Cash pulled back and looked him in the eyes. He was still so handsome, and his locks had grown much longer. He had a few grey strands in his beard, but it made him sexier.

"I've been missing you for almost two decades," Nino responded, and it made Cash's heart flutter.

"I've missed you too."

A whoosh of sadness flowed through her body. She took the back of her hand and brushed across his face as she watched him endearingly. Couldn't no one tell Cash she wasn't living in a dream, and for days she'd pinch herself to wake up.

Nino too had been glued to the windowpane waiting on his wife's arrival anytime she'd texted that she was coming by. The days spent together were surreal, and the nights she had to go were despairing. Most mornings, Cash would wake up cuddled in the arms of Nino where she found peace. Nino would spend most of those nights sleepless because he too couldn't believe it. Finally, after so many years, Nino felt alive. He didn't feel like Abdullah Hassan. He felt like Brooklyn Carter, the man that once had a purpose of living. Sex was the last thing on either of their minds; they were just happy to be together.

"Hey, Cash. What you two kids up to?" Doctor Stine stuck his head into Nino's bedroom door.

"Hey, David." Cash called him by his first name and smiled politely.

Since the day she had discovered Nino, all her enraged thoughts of the Doctor had gone away. They talked about the movie and even a book he was writing. Because the Doctor had saved Nino's life, Cash decided to let him continue his projects without any legal documentation.

"I'm actually glad you're here. Is it possible we can meet this weekend to go over some things for the book?" Doctor asked eagerly, in hopes that she would agree.

Halo had officially earned $2.642 billion dollars and counting at the worldwide box office. It was, of course, a huge cultural phenomenon, but what the world didn't know was, it was based on a true story. Doctor Stine was excited to write the novel to go with the movie, so he'd spent countless nights researching the media's information about the Lopez Cartel. Now that he had Cash Lopez in the flesh, he knew he could make twice as much, and a record breaking amount with a novel that continues *Life After Love.*

"Umm, sure. We can meet down at the beach if you don't mind driving?"

"Of course, not." Doctor Stine was excited.

"Hey, Mrs. Stine." Cash spoke to Charlotte as she walked past the room.

When Charlotte noticed it was Cash, she turned her nose up but she did speak. "Cash," was all she said before her eyes landed on Nino.

Feeling the guilt of sleeping with Mrs. Stine, Nino tried hard to ignore her. However, Doctor Stine was already aware of the affair, and Cash felt something in the pit of her stomach. Cash was no fool. She was not only nice to the two, and she had spared the doctor's life. However, she paid close attention to the way Charlotte would look at Nino blissfully with a hint of jealousy.

"Okay. Well, we're gonna run along. Cash, I'll see you in a few days," David informed Cash because he felt the awkward moment. Right now, he didn't need Charlotte messing things up for him. He needed Cash and Nino in his good graces until everything in his story unfolded.

When Doctor Stine and Charlotte left the room, Cash removed her wet clothing and snuggled under Nino by the window. They both began to watch the rain, and they both fell into a daze. The sound of Cash's phone began to ring, and she cursed under her breath because she meant to turn it off. She pulled it from her purse, and when she noticed it was Kellz, guilt began to consume her.

"One of yo' little niggas?" Nino asked, slightly jealous. He knew deep down that there was someone occupying Cash's time, but because it had been so many years, he really couldn't be mad.

"No, it wasn't a nigga."

"Cash, a nigga ain't dumb, ma," Nino said, then looked out the window for a brief moment. "It's been so many years, I can't even be mad. But I will say this. Whatever you got going, you need to dead that shit soon." Nino finally looked in her direction. "Now if you in love with the nigga, I'll fall back and let you do you. But you need to stop coming around leading me on like we still have a chance." Nino turned to look back out of the window, and Cash didn't have a comeback.

How could she? Nino was right. She was in love with the caller and had been misleading him to believe that there was a possibility. In the back of Nino's mind, this may have been the reason Cash wasn't ready to bring him around, but as he stated, he was gonna give her some time.

"There's nobody, Brook," Cash lied again, then slid under his embrace. Nino wrapped his arms around her and rested his chin on the top of her head. "Let's lay down." Cash spoke above a whisper praying he wouldn't bring up the subject again.

They stood to their feet, then headed over to the bed. Nino stepped out of his sweats and Cash removed her pants. As always Nino rambled through his drawer, then tossed her one of his oversized t-shirts, she slid it on and climbed into the bed to wait for him to join her. When he laid down beside her, he pulled her into his arms and kissed her forehead as he had done every night. Cash let out a deep sigh, and that alone told Nino exactly what he already knew; Cash had someone back at home, and she was protecting his heart.

***

3:26 AM

"Make love to me when my days look low
Pull me in close and don't let me go
Make love to me so when the worlds at war,
That our love heal us all
Help me let down my guard, make love to me, me, me, me, me
Oh, oh make love to me, me, me, me, me..."

Watching Cash as she slept peacefully, Nino was lost in his thoughts. Although they talked and spent time together, Cash was like a complete stranger. He was happy to discover she was alive, but this wasn't the ending he expected. He always dreamed of this day, and in his mind he'd rehearsed exactly what he would say and do to her. He always envisioned making love to her right after she walked down the aisle for the third time. In Nino's heart, the third time was always a charm, and he promised himself if God ever gave him the chance, this time things would be right. Nino had spent plenty of sleepless nights having this same dream, which was why he was awake now.

Cash's warm body laying next to him kept his dick hard. Her body was still intact after so many years, and her ass was as phat as he had left it. In her sleep, she would snuggle close to him, and he would always ignore temptation. Tonight was a different story. He was trying to figure out a way to make his move without making her feel like he was taking advantage of her. Granted, she was his wife, but because they were still rebuilding, he wanted to take his time.

"Brook." Cash stirred in her sleep and fondly called out to him.

"Yea, ma. I'm right here."

Cash's eyes shot open, and she stared into Nino's eyes blissfully. "Make love to me." She spoke steady and sweetly.

Nino looked at her through the slits of his eyes and like always, his heart began to pound. He wanted to attack her like a K9 dog, but then again, he wanted their first time after a long time to be endearing.

Nino climbed on top of Cash and began kissing her passionately. He traced kisses down her neck to her breasts and her nipples instantly perked up with desire. Cash spread her legs and placed her soft hands on his chest. She was amazed at how ripped he was. Since she'd been back around, she saw the work out that Doctor Stine had him doing, so she understood why he now looked like a WWE wrestler. He had a long scar down his stomach that she traced with the tip of her finger, compliments of the explosion. He also had a scar on the side of his face that slightly led to his neck. The scar actually complimented him because it made him look like a warrior. The life Nino had survived in her eyes he was, indeed, that.

Nino slowly placed the tip of his dick to Cash's opening, and she was already dripping wet. "Relax, wife," Nino coached, because he could feel her legs trembling.

When he slid inside of her, she gasped from forgetting how huge he was down below. After a list of moans, he got fully inside of her and she relaxed. Nino closed his eyes briefly because he needed to savor the moment. He thought of days he and Cash made love, and everything felt like déja vu.

"I love you."

Nino opened his eyes to the sound of her voice. Tears were rolling down her angelic face, and it broke Nino. Not being able to hold back, a lone tear slid down his face, but this didn't stop him. He needed to make love to his wife so he could remind her of the love they once shared. He wanted to remind her of the way he made her feel and the connection they had.

"I love you more."

Nino continued to rotate inside of her with the thrust of his hips. The more he went in and out, he could feel her pussy locking down on him, and it made him bite down into her arm. He wouldn't dare break their eye contact. She moaned, she panted and even cried out in ecstasy. Cash wrapped her legs around his waist pushing him deeper inside of her. She wanted this feeling to last forever in fear of losing him again. She and Nino were both thinking the same thing; they needed their old thing back, and after today, the pot was boiling and their past love flames had risen into a new fire.

CHAPTER 16

KANGO & PAPI

"I know I wasn't there for you, at least I said I'm sorry
You know what it was, I told you that I was heartless
I'm emotionally scarred, that ain't even your fault
But don't listen to them haters tryna fill your ears with salt..."
- Lil Baby

"I think my girl cheating on me."

"Hell nah, nigga."

"For real, Kango. I rolled up to her school today to surprise her with flowers and shit. They said her ass ain't been there. I go to her class, and the teacher says she enrolled but only showed up once."

"Word?" Kango looked at Papi, who shook his head. He looked stressed the fuck out like he was ready to body something. "Yo', something going on with them. I rolled up there about a month ago, and the same shit happened with Fin. She was enrolled for damn sure, but her ass wasn't in class."

"She still not talking to you?"

"Nah."

Kango's jaw clenched just thinking about the way he and Fin ended their relationship. After the night at the club, Fin called for days, but Kango wouldn't answer. When he finally decided to call and make amends, Fin's number was changed. He went by Cash's crib to see her, and she wouldn't talk to him. She had cut him off, and now he regretted what had taken place between them. All he was trying to do was teach Fin a lesson, and everything backfired on him.

"I swear that bitch dead if I find out she creeping."

Kango couldn't help but to laugh. He knew Papi meant every word and because of the extent of their relationship he couldn't disagree. They bore a child and had some history. "It's break up season," he added, shaking his head.

"Why you say that?" Papi asked, because Kango and Liyah had him fucked up if they thought he was breaking up. He invested too much into Liyah, and over his dead body would the next nigga reap the benefits.

"Nigga, you ain't noticed yo' moms and Kellz? They barely speak to one another," Kango replied. That was another affair he couldn't help but notice was falling apart. It seemed like these days Jackie was the only one smiling. But he figured she was over the pain with Capone so she found a good head space.

"Damn, I ain't even noticed."

"Yeah, nigga, 'cause you always gone. See, that's where you fucking up. You can't let yo' girl feel lonely when she got a nigga at home. You think shorty cool with you staying out all night while you fucking on strippers and shit?"

"Man, she doesn't know that, though."

"But she assumes. Nine times out of ten, a woman's assumptions are always right."

Papi nodded his head because Kango was right. He noticed how Liyah was so standoffish, and he knew exactly why.

"Where you going, nigga?" Kango asked, because Papi had jumped to his feet and tucked his pistol inside of his pants. They were in the process of counting money, and just like that, Papi flipped.

"Get my bitch."

"From where? You don't even know where she at." Kango burst into laughter.

Papi wanted so bad to curse him out because he was right again. He took a seat feeling foolish, then took a sip from his cup. Kango was doubled over in laughter while Papi mugged him.

"Fuck you laughing for? Goon probably fucking yo' bitch right now," Papi shot across the table.

Kango looked at him seriously, then jumped to his feet. He did the same as Papi and grabbed his gun from the table. Now it was Papi's turn to die in laughter. Kango looked at him, and he couldn't help but laugh along. "Stop playing with me, hoe."

They both shared a laugh and continued counting the few hundred grand that sat in front of them.

"It's nine in the morning, and these chicks got a nigga drinking Hennessy looking like lost puppies." Papi shook his head. He then looked down at his watch for the tenth time in the last thirty minutes. "The shop. It opens at ten."

"Then why the fuck we here?" Kango shot to his feet and they grabbed their guns.

They left the money right there with no worries. Every dollar would be counted for no matter how long it took them to come back. They walked out of the house, and right when they got outside, Cash was pulling into the gate.

Instead of climbing into the car, Papi waited for her to park and get out. "Where the fuck you been?" he asked her the moment she walked over to him.

"Boy, mind yo' damn business." Cash waved him off.

"You is my business, and a'ight. I ain't gon' get Kellz off yo' ass when he beating yo' ass."

"Kellz ain't gon' do shit."

"Yeah, we gon' see. Take yo' ass in there smelling like Axe if you want too." Papi shook his head. He was no fool. His mother was on some fuck shit, and this explained why Kango said her and Kellz weren't speaking.

Cash stopped as if she had been caught. She was a bit skittish to walk inside because if Papi smelled it, then Kellz would definitely catch a whiff of her.

"He ain't here." Papi shook his head, relieving her.

Cash let out a sigh, then went into the house to shower.

Kango and Papi hopped into the vehicle to head for the shop. Papi's thoughts of Liyah cheating was pushed to the back of the mind because he was now puzzled as to whom his mother was having an affair with. He didn't trust niggas with Cash. There was always a motive, and after the stories he'd heard, he was very overprotective. Not to mention he loved Kellz dearly, and he would never wanna see him hurt. He didn't know the problems they were having, but he was gonna make sure to get in his mother's ass when he got back. Kellz was a good dude, and he ain't wanna see his mother fumble the ball.

***

When Kango and Papi pulled up to the shop, Enfinity's brand new white on white Maserati truck had just pulled up front. Kango watched as she climbed out with a pair of shades hovering her eyes. She hopped out looking like a million dollars, and this was something else Kango noticed. She had a new whip, was rocking AP watches and her clothing was overpriced. Many times he'd tried to cop Fin plenty of clothing, jewelry and anything to change up her appearance, and she would always decline. She accepted a few things here and there, but she always complained about having her own money. When Papi told Kango Fin had cashed him out for the shop, it took him by surprise. He wondered if she met her a nigga that was lacing her.

"Damn, nigga. You gon' just stare at her or say something?" Papi laughed, bringing Kango from his daze. "Where yo' friend at?" he then asked, beating Kango to the punch as they approached Fin.

"She here already," Fin stopped to respond.

"And where yo' ass been?" Kango frowned.

"None of your fucking business." Fin walked into the shop in annoyance.

Kango was right on her heels. He followed her to her office, but he examined the entire shop on the way. He was impressed. She had remodeled and furnished the entire shop in only a month. She had a pink, black and white scheme going that looked good. It hurt him to be standing inside her establishment, and he wasn't with her to share her success.

"What the fuck, Kango?" Fin spewed because she wasn't up for his bullshit.

"You did a great job with the shop, shorty. A nigga proud of you."

"Thank you," Fin replied, and began scrolling through her phone.

Goon: *I'm pulling up in ten.*

Fin smiled reading the text from Goon. In another life, she would have shit bricks knowing Goon was coming while Kango was there. However, because of the stunt he pulled with the stripper, she wanted him to see she wasn't sweating him. It was his fault. Had he not been on some bullshit, Fin wouldn't be entertaining another nigga. Simple.

"That's yo' little nigga?" Kango asked, grabbing Fin's attention.

"I ain't got no nigga, and I ain't worried 'bout no nigga right now," Fin half-ass lied. Her and Goon texted from time to time, and he'd dropped by a few times to bring her lunch. She liked Goon, but right now, she was focusing on herself. Her and Liyah had a secret empire to run. Therefore, she didn't need any distractions. The only thing that distracted her were thoughts of Kango. She couldn't front, she missed him like crazy.

"So how you get the bread to cop all this?" Kango looked around the shop, then to the AP she was rocking. The watch was well over three hundred grand, and Kango knew this because he owned several. Now, Liyah's new whip and anything she copped wouldn't surprise him because the girl was paid. But, Fin, nah. She was tangled into something out of her ordinary.

"Cash," Fin replied quickly before he could say anything else.

Kango watched her momentarily, but he left it alone. Suddenly, the sound of arguing caught their attention. Fin jumped to her feet, and they both raced into the salon. When they ran in, Liyah was on top of Kosha dragging her through the shop. Papi was trying to break them up, but Liyah was going crazy.

"What the fuck, yo'!" Kango snatched Kosho from under Liyah, and Papi pulled Liyah back.

"Yeah, bitch, disrespect me again and I'mma show you why you don't wanna fuck with me! Papi, you better get yo' little bitch up outta here!" Liyah snapped.

Knowing what Liyah would possibly do to Kosho, he pulled her out of the shop to protect her. This was a norm for Liyah and Papi. She'd always find herself having to put paws on one of Papi's bitches. And after, she'd remind them not only could she fight, but she could shoot.

"She gon' get hers. Watch." Kosho tugged at a loose piece of hair hanging down in the front of her face. Her lip was beginning to swell, and she had a knot on the side of her head the size of a golf ball.

"Shorty, you don't want them problems. Just roll, ma, because next time, I ain't gon' be able to stop her," Kango assured her.

Kosho wanted so badly to pop off, but after the ass beating she had just gotten, she decided to get ghost. She ran to her car in full speed, and the shit made Kango laugh. He cracked up to himself as he headed back into the shop but stopped in his tracks when he noticed Goon walking in with Wingstop. *I know this nigga ain't...*

CHAPTER 17

ENFINITY

"Well, I never meant to cause you no pain.
I just wanna go back to being the same.
And I only wanna make things right
Before you walk out of my life..."
-Monica

After everything that transpired, Fin became nervous the moment she noticed Goon walking through the door. Her palms began to sweat, and when she saw the mean mug Kango was wearing, she was rattled. Kango was right behind Goon as he sat the food down on one of the stations. Goon walked over to slap hands with Papi, and when he turned around, Kango was right there.

"Sup, Kango?" Goon spoke, but Kango didn't reply. "Sup with this nigga?" Goon looked at Papi.

"What's up with you, nigga?"

"Man, come on, Kango. We boys." Goon threw his hands up.

"You ain't my boy."

"Y'all, don't start this shit." Papi shook his head.

"Man, fuck dude." Kango waved him off. "So you fuck with dude or what?" He looked over to Fin.

She bit into her lip nervously, but she wasn't gonna make fake accusations. "No, Kango. We're just friends."

"Yeah, a'ight." Kango walked out of the door.

Goon stood frozen watching him. He wasn't scared; he just didn't need the confrontation with Kango because they had to pretty much work together. Kango and Papi had basically become partners, and because Goon worked for Papi, he didn't need the heat.

"Aye, yo', you gotta figure this shit out, Fin. You say you and ole' boy done, but, shit, I can't tell. I'm not about to be beefing over you on the strength of Papi. I'mma back up until you figure this shit out, ma." Just like Kango, Goon strolled right on out the door and climbed into his car.

Papi continued to shake his head because it wasn't his business. However, he refused to let them go to war over a female. Fin and Kango were now over, but he knew better; Kango wasn't letting go that easy. Goon, on the other hand, wasn't wrong because Fin was free game.

"He right, ma. You gotta figure this shit out," Papi told Fin, hoping she'd make up her mind soon. Goon was his boy, but Kango had become like family. The relationship between Jackie and Cash made their bond stronger. Therefore, if Kango bodied Goon, it would be out of his control.

"Shut the fuck up, hoe. You got your fucking nerves," Liyah shot across the room with an eye roll.

Fin laughed apprehensively because she was still a bit shaky.

"Man, bring yo' ass here." Papi walked over to Liyah and playful put her in a headlock.

Fin looked over to the food Goon had brought, but she pretty much lost her appetite. She was not only embarrassed, she was confused. At this point, she wanted to wave the white flag with Kango. After giving it some thought, she made up her mind to end the friendship with Goon and give Kango a chance. She pulled her phone from the table and placed a text. She nervously waited for Kango to reply, and when he did, she smiled relieved. The two began to text back and forth until they agreed to go out and talk. They both had hurt one another, and it was time to repair. She was gonna put everything behind her and give the man that deserved her love another chance.

***

On the drive to the warehouse, per usual, Fin and Liyah were jamming to one of City Girls' hit songs. They were so in tune with the music they never noticed the car that trailed behind them. The two pulled up to the warehouse and climbed out to begin the day's work. When they walked in, Timothy and the few men they hired were already in the swing of things. The girls split up and went to their stations and slid into their lab coats and goggles. The music from above played through the warehouse, and everyone was pretty much in their own world. Fin, who was now comfortable, danced along as she poured her contents into the flask. She turned on the fire and watched in awe. This was always her favorite part.

"So this what y'all been up too."

Everyone stopped to look up, and Fin's heart sank. Jackie stood there with her arms crossed in disbelief. Fin nervously looked over to Liyah, and she too was shocked that they had been caught.

"Oh, shit," Liyah said, and began scrambling as if she could hide what they were doing.

Fin and Jackie locked eyes momentarily until Jackie walked over to where she stood and began examining the contents in front of her. Fin dropped her head in shame because she knew Jackie would tell Cash. She let out a deep sigh afraid to look in her direction.

"Enfinity, now you know better." Jackie shook her head. Regardless of how Fin felt about her at this moment, she was disappointed. "Get over here, little girl." She motioned for Liyah. When they both stood in front of her she couldn't only shake her head. "Now y'all know I'm not gonna tell Cash. However, y'all gotta figure this shit out. This was something we didn't want from you guys. Fin, I know you're upset with me, but this shit is a prime example why you can't judge someone's behavior. You judged me and my actions that I'm not proud of, but you're damn near doing the same shit." Jackie looked around in awe. The warehouse looked like some shit out of a movie.

These girls got a whole damn operation going on, Jackie thought. "What if something had happened to you girls, and we don't know shit?" She looked at both girls. "And who are you? Let me guess. You're the mastermind behind this?" Jackie looked over to Timothy, who looked scared as if he was caught by his own parents. When he didn't reply, Jackie knew it was true. Again, she shook her head and began rubbing her stomach. The chemicals were a bit strong, so she decided to leave. She walked over to the door, but before she walked out, she turned to look at the girls who still looked on nervously. "For future references, make sure y'all check your surroundings. City Girls ain't that damn important." She shook her head and walked out.

The girls looked at one another, and they both couldn't believe they were so loose with their operations. Jackie could have been anybody. By the grace of God it was Jackie and not the police; or even worse, Cash.

"Damn, we slipping, man," Liyah told Fin and headed back over to her station. Although she mentioned not telling Cash, she knew one day it would come up. It was time Fin and Liyah changed up their program.

"I mean, she's right. We don't need to be here anymore, Liyah. We can have Timothy and the fellas cook. We'll just have to up their pay."

"I'm with it. I can't risk Cash or Papi finding out. Both their ass would kill me." Liyah swooped her hair behind her ear. "I know you not feeling Jackie, but this might be the time you talk to her. I mean, she's right. You judge her character because of her street behavior, and this the same shit. No, we were not killing people, but eventually, we might have too. Let's just say Timothy stole from us. You think we'll let him live?"

"Woooo," Timothy said, making everyone laugh.

"Not like that, Tim. But real shit." Liyah looked from Tim

back to Fin. "Then you find out Timothy was Kango's brother." Liyah tried to make a valid point.

"He's white," Fin added.

"Man, you know what the fuck I mean."

They both laughed.

"No I feel you." Fin dropped her head. She knew it was time her and Jackie had that talk. She had already contemplated expressing herself to Jackie, but now she had no choice.

"Let's get this shit done so we can go. This week we will have a meeting with the guys and get things squared away."

"Okay." Fin nodded and began working. Between Kango and Jackie, Fin's mind was clouded.

CHAPTER 18

DOCTOR STINE

"After the pain, you come and love me
And I welcome you, you're a glad sight to see
And after the rain and all that I have been through
I still can't explain how I can still love you like I do..."
- Betty Wright

Doctor Stine pressed send on his last email that had to be sent to his editor. He spun around in his office chair flushed with excitement. He had pressed The End on part two of his novel titled Life After Love. He wanted so badly to dive into part three of the story, but he was gonna wait to see how things would pan out with Cash and Nino. Because part three would be the ending of his story, he needed it to be actioned so he could go out with a bang. He hadn't yet contemplated an ending for the story, but in due time, he would come up with something to leave a reader's jaw dropping.

Cash agreeing to let him continue his story of their lives was the most electrifying thing a person could do for his career. After the reincarnation of Nino, and *Halo* being the number one selling movie of all times, Doctor Stine hung up his lab coat. He resigned from being a doctor because he had enough money to live forever. If he thought he found passion in being a doctor, he was misconstrued because his passion was now into book writing and films.

Over the course of time, Doctor Stine had become obsessed with the life of Cash Lopez. He spent many sleepless nights trapped inside of his home office with a cup of coffee and an adrenaline rush. Right now he was ecstatic about meeting with Cash Lopez today, so he powered off his computer and grabbed his laptop. He began packing his belongings, then headed to his bedroom. When he walked in, Charlotte was laying in her bed under the weather.

"I'll see you later, honey." He forced a smile, then kissed her cheek.

Doctor Stine was no fool. He knew exactly why the long face, and she had been mopping for the last month or so. All because of Brooklyn Nino. Now that Cash was back, Nino deprived her of sex, and he couldn't blame him. What did Charlotte have on Cash Lopez? Not a damn thing. Cash was not only beautiful, but she had the sex appeal to lure in any man that crossed her path.

"I'll see you," Charlotte replied dryly.

Doctor Stine snickered under his breath. He couldn't wait until this book was over with because he was filing for a divorce. He thanked God they bore no children, and he was happy he had money before they were married. Charlotte couldn't get him for a dime, and he would for sure send her walking with the same bag of clothing she came with.

Doctor Stine headed out the door and to his car. Just as he climbed in, his phone began to ring with an unknown number. It was a 323 area code, which told him the caller was calling from California. He sat his belongings down and answered the call. "Doctor," was his greeting, and he waited to hear the callers voice.

"Hello, Doctor Stine?"

"That would be me. May I ask who I'm speaking with?"

"Ummm..." The caller paused without introduction. "I'm...I'm calling because I have some information that would help your book."

"My book?"

"Yes. I saw your movie and read your book. Trust me, I have some juice for your story."

"Oh, I see. And what ties do you have to Cash Lopez?"

"Oh, trust me. By the time I'm done telling you my story, you'll be able to write a spinoff."

Hearing these words were magic to Doctor Stine's ears. He really didn't wanna stop at book three, but he knew the story would eventually have to come to an end.

"Well, we can meet if you're able to. How's next weekend?"

"I'm game."

"Okay, and is this your number?"

"Yes. Call me to confirm, and thank you."

"Oh, thank you." Doctor ended the call, and he was more exhilarated.

The caller had to know Cash and her peers because anyone in the world that saw that movie would only know the story is about Cash if they knew her story. He started his engine and headed for the highway. He wasn't gonna mention the call to Cash until after the meeting with the caller. He knew there could be a conflict of interest, so he was gonna keep the info to himself.

***

"Oh my God, Doctor Stine." Cash laughed as she covered her mouth bashfully.

"So how was it? Come on, Cash, I have to know this stuff. I need to know your emotions, what taints you, what's magical, your dislikes...stuff like that."

"I understand, and, yes, you said the right word." Cash stopped and looked at David as she called him. "Nino. Nino is magical. It was memorable, and if I said I didn't miss that man, I'd be a damn lie...Can I ask you a question, Doctor Stine?" Cash asked sarcastically.

"Sure."

"What made you tell my story?"

Doctor Stine looked at Cash, then reached over to mute the recorder. "Off the record, everyone knew The Lopez Cartel. Let's just say I knew your mother well. Cash, I've been a doctor for years, and I've done work for some major league people."

"So you know..."

"Braxton?" Cash and David spoke at the same time.

David nodded yes. "Does Nino know?"

"No." Cash dropped her head in shame. She was relieved Nino didn't know of Braxton and Skylar. She knew eventually she would have to tell him, but now wasn't the time.

"Tell me, Cash." David pushed the record button on the recorder. "Do you plan on telling him about Sky?"

Cash looked at David astounded that he knew of her child's name and that he was recording.

"I have no choice."

Doctor Stine wanted badly to ask about BJ, but he chose not to. He knew if he asked, it would only open a can of worms he wasn't ready to tell. The truth of the matter was, Doctor Stine knew all about BJ being alive. He also knew about Liyah and everything she was tied into. Something he had chosen to leave out to protect Cash's demise. He knew of the beef between both Cartels. Once upon a time, he and Braxton did house calls for Mario, who was the leader of the Carlito Cartel that Ms. Lopez beefed with. Each time he stitched up one of their henchmen, Ms. Lopez's crew was always responsible.

CHAPTER 19

BROOKLYN JR. (PAPI)

"Sometimes I miss my dad, I wish he could see me now
Rolls Royce, he wouldn't believe me now
The way I took my mom out the hood, got Tweety round
From the jects to the burbs, I wish you could meet me now..."
- Meek Mill

"Local officials are trying to crack down on a high volume of Methamphetamine that has surged throughout the United States. The meth cases have been overwhelming for local police across the state and could be hazardous to teens. Methamphetamine is now the primary drug flooding the streets of Greater Miami and other communities across the country. Our local departments are trying to do everything they can to put the madness to an end. We'll have more on this story coming up."

"Damn." Papi shook his head as he watched the news. He looked over to Liyah, who sat on bed with her legs crossed.

What Papi didn't know was, her heart was racing and she knew exactly who the news was referring too. In so little time, her and Fin had the streets of Miami filled up with meth. She didn't quite know what the news meant, but she was gonna reach out to Lexington, who was in their pockets and worked for Miami PD.

"Man I just need to know who the fuck that is. I might need to get in the meth game," Papi boasted. He stood to his feet and prepared to walk out of the room. He needed to go to talk to his mother.

As he made his way into the hall, Skylar was coming out of her bedroom. She noticed her brother and became excited. She loved Papi, and he loved her back.

"Are you Papi today or BJ? Sometimes mom calls you Papi, and sometimes she calls you BJ."

"I'm always BJ to you, Sky." Papi laughed. She was the only one that could get away with calling him BJ.

"Okay. Well, BJ, come see what I built." Skylar pulled BJ into her bedroom.

Being the big brother he was, BJ followed Skylar into her princess castle as she called it. When he walked in, he didn't know what to expect. However, he was applauded. There was a tunnel sitting on her desk with some sort of device. He looked at the small box she held that looked like a remote.

"Sky, what is this?"

"A bomb," Skylar responded with a shoulder shrug.

"A bomb? What you mean a bomb?"

"It's a bomb. If you pull this, it will explode. Don't pull it," Skylar replied seriously.

"Lil' Ma, why do you have a bomb? Wait...why did you build a bomb?" Papi asked worriedly.

"Mommy," Skylar replied, and began working on her project as if it was nothing.

For the life of him, he didn't understand what the fuck just happened. "Good job, baby girl." He and Skylar did their normal high five, but he was still blown back.

"Thanks." Skylar smiled proudly.

Papi shook his head and headed out of the princess castle. He turned right into his mother's bedroom and found Cash laying on her bed looking at the TV. He could tell she wasn't watching the TV; it was pretty much watching her as she appeared to be in deep thought.

"Ma."

"Hey, Papi."

"Where's Kellz?"

"He's out handling business," Cash replied nonchalantly. "What's up with you?" Cash looked at Papi, and she could tell something was bothering him. With her better judgement, she figured it had something to do with her and Kellz. Therefore, she remained quiet.

"Ma, you been on some shit lately. Who dis nigga you been seeing?" Papi got right to the point.

Cash observed his body language, and because she was prepared for him to ask, she kept her game face on. "I have something I need you to see." A flush of nervousness mixed with excitement ran through Cash's body. It was time. She lifted from the bed and let out a small sigh. She slid into her slippers and grabbed her keys from the dresser. She then motioned for Papi to follow, and they headed out to Cash's vehicle. "Okay, look. What I'm about to show you is not only crazy, but it's life changing. Whatever you do, don't mention anything about our lives here back at home. And whatever you do, don't mention anything about what I'm gonna show you to anyone back here at home." Cash looked over before pulling off.

"Ma, you scaring me."

"There's nothing to be scared about, son," Cash replied, and Papi relaxed in his seat.

Cash started the car and they pulled out of the spiral gates. The entire way to the highway, Papi noticed how quiet his mother was and wondered what she had to show him. Whatever it was, it was serious. He was a bit nervous and over-whelmed, and Cash wasn't making things any better. She continued to tell him to relax, but how could he when she was fidgeting in her seat?

After the two hour flight on Cash's private jet, Cash and Papi climbed into the vehicle that awaited them. They drove out thirty minutes or so, then pulled up to the home. Cash slug-

114

gishly let out a deep sigh, then instructed Papi to get out and follow. When Papi stepped out, he observed the huge home wondering who the home belonged to. When they made it to the door, Charlotte smiled at Papi, then gave Cash a half-ass smile. Cash rolled her eyes and stepped past Charlotte because she was tired of being polite.

"Wait here, son," Cash told Papi, then headed towards the back of the home.

"You must be Abdullah's son. Oh, my, you look just like him." Charlotte was stunned at how much the two looked alike. She watched Papi closely because not only did he look like Nino, he was just as handsome.

"Abdullah?" Papi frowned. Before he could finish, he heard the sound of his mother's voice.

"Just come here. I have someone I want you to see." When they came into view, Papi's eyes widened. He watched his father stroll through the foyer, and he was huge.

"BJ?" Nino asked, looking from Cash to Papi.

Tears had already trickled down Cash's face as she watched her husband and son standing in the same room. That same feeling she had when she first saw Nino came rushing back, and she couldn't contain her tears.

"Pops?" Papi did the same as Nino. He looked from his father to his mother, then back to his father in an unbelievable state. For the first time in years, several tears began to fall from Papi's eyes. He ran into his arms, and Nino hugged him strongly. They embraced for what felt like an eternity before letting each other go. "Damn, this is crazy." Papi was still aghast. "How... When...? Man, this some crazy shit, dawg." Papi shook his head. "So this where yo' fast ass been?" Papi looked over to Cash, and they all burst out into laughter. "I knew it." He chuckled.

"This where I been creeping to," Cash added.

Papi looked at her, and Kellz crossed his mind. He wondered to himself how she was gonna pull this one off. As stated, he liked Kellz, but this was his father. *Bye Lance*, he thought to himself and smiled. This was the happiest moment of his entire life, and nothing or no one could steal his joy. He couldn't wait until his Pops was back home, and their lives could begin.

CHAPTER 20

KELLZ

"I got this feeling, and I just can't turn it loose
That somebody's been getting next to you
I don't want to walk around knowin' I was your fool
'Cause being the man that I am, I just can't lose my cool..."
- Dru Hill

"Y ou gotta be lying. Bitch, so what you gonna do? Are you gonna be with him?"

"I don't know, Jackie. I mean, yeah, but I have too..." Before Cash could finish, Kellz walked into the room. They both got quiet, and it rubbed Kellz wrong.

"Hey, Kelly." Cash smiled in hopes he wouldn't dissect what they had been talking about.

"Sup, baby? Sup, Jack?" Kellz walked over and kissed Cash on the cheek.

"You hungry? Chef whipped up some Cornish hens and greens."

"Yeah, I'mma go shower real quick. Have 'em make my plate, and I'll be back down."

"Okay," Cash replied, and Kellz strolled off and headed upstairs.

When he got to his room, he stripped from his clothing that he was sure smelled like Drina. Since he and Cash had been on bad terms, he was spending more time with his ex-wife and children. He didn't plan on leaving Cash. He was just busying himself to keep from stressing. He couldn't front. He was having fun with Drina, but she was no Cash. Cash Lopez was the type of chick that was heaven sent. Comparing her to a dime a dozen would be an understatement because they stopped making women like her when they made her.

At this point, Kellz wanted things to work between the two. He just felt the need to give Cash some time. He spent lonely nights wondering if she was sleeping in somebody else's bed. It hurt his soul to have these thoughts, and the foul play was from what had been transpiring here lately. Every day he'd been coming home, Cash had been MIA. He would always just shower and spend time with Skylar. At times, he would call Cash, and either her phone would be powered off, or she wouldn't answer. When she did answer, she'd sound whispery.

After listening to what her and Jackie discussed, it made him wonder who they referred to. For the first time, he wanted to do some investigation. He thought of putting a tracking device on her vehicle but quickly thought against it because he knew what Cash was capable of.

After washing up and stepping out of the shower, Kellz went into his room to dry off. When he walked into his bedroom, he was startled because Cash was standing over by the dresser with his phone in her hand. He became nervous because he hadn't erased the messages between him and Drina.

"Your phone was going off. It's Drina." Cash handed Kellz his phone. He looked at her timidly. He took the phone from her hand and looked at the call.

"She don't want shit. The kids need money for cheer," he lied, and sat the phone back down on the dresser.

Cash rolled her eyes on the sly, but she couldn't help to eyeball Kellz in his towel. The bulge in the front of his towel and the water that still glistened on his body turned her on. Kellz watched her eyes and was relieved this was his way to escape his guilt.

"You eyeing a nigga like you ain't never seen dick like this." Kellz smirked and un-wrapped his towel.

Cash watched him with hunger because she hadn't had any in weeks. Little did Kellz know, Cash had seen dick better. No man topped Nino in the dick department. The way he was fucking her left her delirious. Kellz wasn't bad in the sex department, but he wasn't Nino. It reminded Cash why she chose to carry his last name. That man had taken her body to heights that no man had even taken her to.

Cash walked over to Kellz and grabbed a handful of dick. She looked into his eyes and smirked. Kellz's heart began to thump because he was happy Cash was giving him this much attention. She began stroking his manhood until she couldn't take it anymore. With one hand, she continued to stroke him, and with the next, she undressed. In no time, Kellz's dick stood at attention, ready for Miss Cash to put her world famous pussy on him. For days, Kellz had waited for this moment in hunger. He was so eager to make love to her, so he snatched her up aggressively and laid her back on the bed.

He then lifted both her legs into the air, taking them into the palm of his hand, and without help, he inserted himself inside of her. Kellz used only his waist to cause a wave of motion as he looked her in the eyes. He didn't know if he was tripping or not, but she didn't have that same look of admiration in her eyes. She looked despairing as if something was hurting her. She looked confused as if Kellz was a total stranger. His heart began to hurt, and he knew now for sure Cash was slipping away from him. *But how? And why?*

"I love you, Cash." Kellz spoke somberly as if he needed to remind her.

Instead of replying, a tear cascaded down Cash's face, and her eyes shifted to his chest. She couldn't face him. Thoughts of hurting Kellz haunted her but what hurt more was Nino. She closed her eyes and thought of Nino laying in that room alone. It had been nearly two weeks since Cash last saw Nino. Papi, on the other hand, had been visiting quite frequently. He would lie to

Liyah about going out to hustle, and the girl through fits accusing him of cheating. Cash wanted so bad to inform her of what was going on, but she couldn't risk Kellz finding out. Every day she wrecked her brain with guilt trying to muster up how she would break the news; and although right now was the perfect time, she just couldn't.

"Uhhhhh...Brook, baby..." Cash locked down on Kellz's tool and began to match his stroke.

Just as she was about to release her first nut, Kellz stopped in mid-stroke. Cash's eyes flung open, and Kellz was staring dead at her. He wore a hurt look, and by the wrinkles in his forehead, she could tell he was infuriated.

"You still in love with that nigga, huh?" Kellz lifted from Cash and mugged her.

"No. Who are you talking about?"

"Cash, you just called me, Brook, ma." Kellz shook his head and retrieved his clothing from the ground. He began dressing while Cash tried hard to plead her case. "Just save that shit, ma. Over these last couple months, something about you been off. Normally when we beef, we communicate. Now it's like you don't even give a fuck. I don't know if somebody else got your attention or if that movie really did a number on you, but whatever it is, you need to fix it. I love you, but a nigga like me ain't about to lose his bitch over a muthafucking twenty-year-old memory. I'm out."

Kellz slid into his last shoe and grabbed his keys. He headed for the door, and he expected for Cash to at least say something. Just say she loved him and she didn't wanna lose him. Instead, Cash sat quietly on the bed with her head hanging to the floor. If he had never been hurt before, he was hurt now. Kellz walked out of the room with his heart now on his sleeve. His mind was now made up. He was gonna do something he never thought he'd do in a million years. He needed to know, and after he found out what he needed to find out, he would leave Cash for good.

CHAPTER 21

AALIYAH

"Too strong for too long (and I can't be without you baby)
And I'll be waiting up until you get home
(cuz I can't sleep without you baby)
Anybody who's ever loved, ya know just what I feel
Too hard to fake it, nothing can replace it..."
- Mary J Blige

"I swear if I find out you fucking around, Papi, I'mma fuck the whole Miami up!" Liyah ranted furiously.

She was tired of Papi leaving and not paying attention to her needs. When he did come home, he only played with Escolan, counted his money and ate. He'd be right back out the door. He barely slept, and whatever it was this time, had his undivided attention.

Papi stopped in his tracks to look at Liyah. Normally he'd yoke her up, but right now he didn't have the strength nor the time. Papi was trying to get back to his father. "Liy Liy, look, ma. I know I made some fucked up choices in the past. Shit, even now, but right now, it's not what you think. It's some serious life-changing shit going on, ma. I swear it has nothing to do with a bitch," Papi spoke sincerely. He hated to see Liyah hurt and be fueled by false accusations, but his mother made him swear to never tell a soul.

Liyah paid attention to the candid look in his eyes, and

for the first time, she believed him. She dropped her head shamefully, then picked it up when she felt the soft touch of Papi's hand. He lifted her chin and licked his lips before speaking. Right there in that spot, Liyah melted.

"I love you, lil' girl. I'll be back in a couple days, okay?" Liyah nodded her head yes. "Hopefully by the time I come back, I'll have shit figured out. Liyah, remember I'm not disrespecting this relationship." Papi kissed her cheeks and headed for the door.

"I'll be waiting up for you until you get home."

Liyah put a huge smile on Papi's face. He headed out the door, and Liyah sat in the same spot for some time. For the first time in a long time, she felt a sense of peace. Papi had reassured her heart, and it left her feeling lovingly. Liyah stood to her feet and slid into her clothing. She could go have her meeting with a clear mind. She and Fin were officially putting Timothy and their crew in charge. The only thing they would handle was meeting their connect and distributing the Meth. Liyah pulled her phone from her purse and placed the call to Fin.

"Stopppp, Kango!" Fin giggled into the phone. "Kango, stopppp." Liyah heard the phone drop, and Fin continued with her fit of laughter. Liyah couldn't help but smile happily for Kango and her friend. She loved the two together and was ecstatic they had made up. "Hellooo," Fin cooed into the phone.

"Hey, lover girl. Get yo' ass up. Our meeting starts in two hours."

"I'm up and ready."

"I don't know where you think you going in that outfit," Liyah heard Kango say.

"Don't mind him. He just mad I look good. I'm on my way."

"Okay. I'll meet you there. I'mma leave the house in about forty-five."

"Okay."

Just as they were disconnecting the line Kango's voice blared into the phone. "You gon' suck this dick before you leave."

Liyah ended the call laughing to herself. He sounded like Papi so much it was scary. She continued to get dressed and knew it would take exactly forty-five minutes until she was ready. After this meeting, Liyah could focus on her man. She knew eventually Papi would tell her about whatever he had going on. She chose not to pry, so she was gonna just wait. Liyah loved Papi, and after today, she was sworn in. Nothing could mess up her day, and she was gonna make sure of it.

***

When Liyah pulled into the warehouse, Fin's car was already there. Liyah climbed out feeling like the Boss Bitch she was. If one didn't know any better, they would think she was Cash Lopez. Over the course of years, Liyah had paid close attention to how Cash not only carried herself but how she dressed. Therefore, Liyah was draped in a white mink coat and a pair of Dior shades that covered her eyes. She had on a pair of knee-high boots that held her small 22 LR handgun. She walked into the warehouse with sass and found her newly devoted family sitting on the other side. Because it was a meeting, they weren't gonna meet on the *Lab* side of the room. They were gonna sit at the table just as they had seen in plenty of movies.

"Liy Liy!" Fin called out to her, excited. They hadn't seen each other in a couple days because Fin was spending more time with Kango. She and Jackie hadn't gotten back in tune with one another, but they were cordial enough to speak.

"Finny..." Liyah smiled back and took her seat at the head of the table opposite from Fin. "Tim, Kev, Allen." Liyah spoke to the three men that were a part of their crew. "Where's Brandon?"

"Something came up," Tim replied with a shoulder shrug.

Liyah made a mental note about it because this was a meeting he for sure should have attended. This meeting was important, so if he didn't have a legitimate story, then Liyah would simply cut him off. They had no time for half-steppers, and right now, Brandon looked exactly like that. "Let's go on with this meeting." Liyah removed her coat and placed it on the back of the chair. "As you guys know, we have made a killing. Tim, where are we now?"

"Well, from where we started was about 254 pounds of Methamphetamine, which was about $3.5 million. As of today, we have climbed to 1000 kilograms; an estimated value of $13.5 million," Timothy boasted excitedly.

Everyone began to clap, and Liyah and Fin looked at each other feeling superior.

"I'm a millionaire?" Fin looked at Liyah in disbelief.

Liyah nodded *yes,* and it made her feel great. Although she was the one that copped all of the work, she didn't care. She was happy she could put Fin in a position to get some bread. No matter how much she spent, they were a team.

"Well, as of today, Fin and I will play the background. Timothy will be in charge. We will still come by from time to time to distribute the work to you guys." Liyah got quiet and Fin took the floor.

"We have another warehouse. A truck will be delivering an entire new lab to the new location. This warehouse will be set on fire this weekend, so as of Monday, you guys could go to this location. Take the weekend off." Fin pulled out her phone and sent everyone a text to the new location. Just as she sat her phone down, a text came from an unknown number.

(323) 466-1982: You guys okay?
Enfinity: Jack?
(323) 466-1982: Yes. I was just checking on you girls.
Enfinity: We're fine. Leaving soon. Thank you

Fin knew exactly who it was by the area code. She dropped her phone on the table and looked over at Liyah.

"Who was that?" Liyah asked, sensing something by Fin's facial expression.

"That was Jackie. She was checking up on us."

"Awe. Did you tell her we were good?"

"Yes."

Liyah smiled because she wanted Fin and Jackie to repair their relationship. Just as Cash was with Liyah, Jackie was a mother sent from heaven. She understood why Fin was upset but Jackie loved her dearly. Just like now, she didn't have to check up on them. Not to mention she hadn't told Cash about her discoverance. It was crazy how she knew where they were without asking. This was big to Liyah, and one day, Fin would understand.

CHAPTER 22

CASH LOPEZ

"I put your picture on my mirror
Start to blush when somebody says your name
In my stomach there's a pain
See you walk in my direction I go the other way..."
- Fantasia

It was the day of Nino's birthday, so Cash decided to host a small event with a couple of friends and family. She decided to surprise Nino with Breelah, and she was gonna even bring Aaliyah. It was time, Liyah found out why Papi had been leaving for days at a time. Now who Cash wasn't gonna bring along was Sky. Not only hadn't she told Nino about her, but she was scared Sky would tell Kellz. The two had a dope bond, and Sky had a tendency of running her mouth too much. Often, she'd repeat things she'd heard Papi and Liyah arguing about. Therefore, she decided to leave Skylar with her nanny.

Knock! Knock!

"Come in."

Breelah walked in, and Cash anxiously ran over to hug her. "Breeeeee, I miss you!"

"I miss you too. I'm sorry I've been working so much."

"It's okay. You gotta make that money." Cash smiled. If it was up to her, Breelah wouldn't work a day of her life. But being a lawyer was Breelah's passion, so she wouldn't dare quit.

"Where is that man of yours?" Cash smirked, referring to Young. After all the madness with Que and Mario, everyone was able to breathe peacefully. Young and Breelah had finally hooked up after months of flirting, and they had become pretty serious.

"He's downstairs."

"Good, because I have a surprise for you guys." Cash stopped to look at Breelah. "Breelah, this surprise is gonna be crazy, so grab your tissue, baby."

"I hope it's a good cry."

"Let's just say...very, very overwhelming." Cash nearly wanted to cry right there in the room. She tried hard to contain herself because she knew this was gonna blow Breelah back. "Let's go." Cash tossed her purse over her arm and grabbed her coat. Her and Breelah headed downstairs quickly because Cash didn't want to bump into Skylar. She felt bad she couldn't bring her along, but she just couldn't.

"Hey, Young." Cash smiled widely and gave Young a hug.

"Sup, Boss Lady." Young was happy to see Cash. Since Cash had pretty much got out of the game, Young had decided to leave the game and focus on his family he was trying to start with Breelah. Cash didn't know that Breelah was now with child, but she planned on telling her today.

"Liyah!" Cash called out. "This girl takes forever." Cash was impatient. She couldn't wait to see Nino, and especially the reaction from Breelah.

When Liyah made it down, she embraced Breelah and Young. Young grabbed Escolan from her arms and began raining kisses on his chubby cheeks. They all made their way out the door, then climbed into the SUV to head for the private jet. They all began to make small talk, but every now and then, Cash would zone out.

Liyah noticed and wondered what was on her mind. Liyah had noticed a difference in Cash's demeanor, but she knew Cash was kinda private. It actually confused her because one minute she looked depressed, then the next she was glowing. The way she was acting now, Liyah could tell wherever they were headed had to do with the way she had been smiling. Cash hadn't told Liyah where they were headed, but she did mention Papi would be in attendance. Liyah was excited to see her man, and she was sure he would be happy to see Escolan.

***

Finally arriving at Doctor Stine's home, Cash nervously exited the truck and helped Liyah out with the baby. The balloons caught Breelah's attention; however, it hadn't dawned on her it was her beloved brother's birthday. Once everyone was settled, they headed into the gate. There were nine guards that escorted them into the yard because Cash couldn't take any chances. It seemed that every time something happened, it was a special occasion; like now. This was big, so she was gonna be ten steps ahead. The guards had AR's and wore bulletproof vests. One guard had a bomb strapped to his stomach, and for Cash, he would go out with no regrets.

Cash strolled into the yard like the boss bitch she was wearing her best garments. She needed to remind Nino how she'd become the first lady. This day for Cash was exhilarating, and she had a point to prove. She couldn't wait for the day they could continue what they presented to the world. She wasn't sure how to execute her love story, but right now she was content. Kellz would always cross her mind and how much she'd hurt him. However, she asked herself if he really loved her because he wasn't fighting for her love. After what she had seen in his phone, it only helped her follow her heart. She battled with herself frequently. Was Nino worth it? Of course, so it was time he felt at home.

Cash and the rest of her patrons walked into the yard and were greeted by the servant that had been waiting for their arrival. He escorted Cash to their setting because Cash wanted everything to be a surprise to Nino as well. David had taken him away so that the decorators and caterers could set up. It was shy after 4PM, and Nino was due back at 6:30. Everyone took their seats, and Cash began pouring champagne. Kango, Jackie and Fin would be there shortly, so everything was perfectly designed. Cash was finally able to relax, so she poured a glass of Champagne and sat back to wait patiently.

***

An Hour Later...

Jackie had shown up along with Kango and Enfinity. To Cash's surprise, Fin had actually rode the jet and inside of the car with Jackie. Cash noticed they hadn't said much to one another, but they did indulge in a group chat.

"Mrs. Carter." The host walked over to Cash. "He's here."

"Okay," Cash replied settled, but a hot flash of nervousness flowed through her body.

She then turned to everyone and told them to close their eyes. She quickly walked away and met Nino at the car. He noticed the party set up and couldn't help to smile. However, he didn't know that his biological baby sister was behind the gate, along with his grandson who he hadn't met.

When Cash rounded the corner, she stopped to take in how handsome Nino looked. It was crazy how this man had so much power over her heart. Just seeing him now made her blush just as she did years ago. When he hit her with his sexy smile, she melted into a puddle right there along the grass. He then reached out his arms, and she ran over to him graciously.

"Happy Birthday, Husband."

"Thank you, ma. And thanks for all this." Nino looked around and nodded in approval to the guards.

"You're welcome. Now put this on." Cash began tying the blindfold around his eyes.

"Why? You 'bout to take a nigga upstairs and give me some birthday pussy?" Nino smiled.

"Yes. But later." Cash blushed.

Once she was done, she guided him to the back, and the first person she looked at was Breelah. Before Cash took off the blindfold, she began to say a powerful prayer. Instead of Amen, she instructed them to open their eyes. She removed the blindfold from Nino, then looked at Breelah.

"Nino!!!!!!!!" Breelah screamed so loud everyone across the Gulf of Mexico could hear her.

Nino smiled hard, and although Cash had mentioned she had survived, this was their first encounter.

"Bree." Nino's smile lit up the entire sky.

Breelah jumped into his arms with a stream of tears pouring from her eyes. When she finally let go, Nino looked around to the crowd of people and noticed Young. Young was so stunned he froze in one spot with his mouth open. Young looked at Cash, and she hit him with a single head nod. He happily walked over and embraced Nino with so much joy. After they were done with a few short words, Nino walked over to his son and grabbed the baby from his hand.

"This nigga look just like me." Nino smiled. His eyes then darted over to Liyah, who was shy and nervous. She stood back to observe, and it warmed her heart to know this is where Papi had been.

"This is, Liyah. Papi's wife."

"How are you, Liyah? I'm Nino." Nino smiled widely.

Liyah reached out to give him a hug and already her aura won him over.

"You must be Jackie, Fin and Kango." Nino addressed. Everyone nodded their heads. He gave the ladies hugs, then shook hands with Kango. "I've heard so much about y'all. Man, Cash really rocks with y'all heavy. And you." He stopped to point to Jackie. "You a wild one." Everyone laughed.

Everyone began badgering Nino with question after question. Shortly after, Doctor Stine walked over and everyone greeted him. For the rest of the day, they all enjoyed the party with drinks, laughter and even danced on the makeshift dance floor. This would be a day to remember, and especially for Bree who was still in total disbelief. The energy in the front yard was electrifying, and when Breelah announced her pregnancy, they all did a toast and congratulated her and Young.

CHAPTER 23

KELLZ

"I know the way a nigga livin' was whack
But you don't get a nigga back like that!
Shit I'm a man with pride, you don't do shit like that
You don't just pick up and leave and leave me sick like that..."
- Jay Z

After leaving Drina's house, Kellz climbed into his car and headed home. He and Drina had made love all morning, and for the first time, he was feeling guilty. He left Drina in the once bedroom that they shared in a pool of tears. He told her he couldn't do it anymore and he had to get his girl back. Therefore, he raced down the highway home in hopes that Cash was there. He couldn't take another day without her because he was slowly dying inside. Cash meant the world to Kellz, and her love was worth fighting for. He was very familiar with Cash's ways, and one thing she hated was a weak nigga. He could imagine how he looked to her at this point because instead of putting his foot down, he was giving up; biggest sign of weakness.

When Kellz pulled up to the house, all Cash's vehicles were aligned outside, so he sighed in relief that she was home. He exited the car and picked up the three dozen white roses in his passenger's seat before heading into the home. He went straight upstairs to find his bedroom empty and a note laying on the bed. Kellz walked over to the bed and picked up the note.

I'll be stepping out for a couple days.
When I get back, we need to talk, and it's really important.

-Cash

It was all the note read and something tugged at his heart. It was something about the way he read it that told him something wasn't right when she wrote it. Too eager to wait, Kellz dialed her number in hopes they could talk now. When she didn't answer, he shook his head and it only pained him more. Kellz lifted from the bed and headed up the hall. Just as he made it to the staircasing, Skylar began screaming his name.

"Kellz! Kellz! Kellz!" Skylar ran over happy to see him.

"Hey, baby girl." Kellz swooped Sky into his arms and kissed her forehead. "What you doing, ma? You miss me?"

"Yes, I miss you. Can you stay with me? I'm tired of being here alone."

"Alone? Where's everybody at?"

"They all got dressed and left."

"And why didn't you go?"

"Mommy said I couldn't go because I run my mouth too much." Skylar sighed dramatically.

"Okay. Well, go get yo' shoes. You can roll with me." Kellz put Sky down and she ran off to get her shoes. It was time Kellz took matters into his own hands. He pulled out his tracking device and pulled up Cash's location. He knew if she found out he was tracking her she would lose her cool, especially because this was something Que had done in the past. Cash always mentioned how she hated people keeping tabs on her, but right now Kellz didn't give a fuck. When the red dot pin-pointed to her location, it showed him that she was in the Gulf of Mexico.

Cash always mentioned she had to fly out to meet her new connect, so Kellz figured that was where she'd been. Plenty times Kellz watched her location, and she would always be in

133

the same spot. Even the days she didn't come home. Now that Skylar had mentioned her getting dolled up, it made him wonder if she was sleeping with this *new connect*. Cash was no angel, and he knew this first hand. Therefore, he didn't put shit past her no matter how much older she had gotten. One thing he would never do was interfere with her business, and that was where she always won. But something told him there was some foul shit going on.

Just as Kellz turned to leave, Sky came running up the hall with her purse on. Kellz couldn't help but smile because she was such a little lady. She was a split imagine of Cash, and the only difference was the dimple. Kellz wanted so badly to tell her he'd be back, but the gleam in her eyes of leaving made him feel obligated to take her. She was already let down because everyone had left her out, so Kellz couldn't bring himself to break her heart. He grabbed her tiny hands, and with his free hand, he dialed the number to the port where Cash's private jet was located.

"Mr. Cook, I need to get flown out on the jet. Gulf of Mexico."

"I'm sorry, Mr. Scott, but Ms. Lopez is on the jet."

"Well, get me a copter. I don't care what it is, it better be there by the time I make it." Kellz ended the call and headed for the car with Skylar by his side.

He looked down at the child and tried to figure out how he could keep her from getting harmed. He wasn't sure what he would be getting himself into, so he had to think quickly. Whatever it was, he prayed to the grace of God that his mind was playing tricks on him. He didn't want him and Cash's love affair to end. He didn't want Drina, and he didn't want the many women in Miami. He wanted Cash Lopez; the lady he fell in love with over time.

"Kelly, are you okay?" Skylar asked, noticing how Kellz closed his eyes to meditate to himself. He let out a sigh and looked down at Skylar. He couldn't help but smile because she looked concerned.

"I'm okay, lil' ma. I'm okay," he assured her and she smiled back. However, he wasn't okay, and soon he would be assured.

***

"Ooh, a party." Skylar lifted up in her seat and looked out the window.

Instead of Kellz having the helicopter to take him to the port, he directed the pilot to the location on his tracker. When he made it to the location, they searched for somewhere to land. The yard was so huge he decided to just land on the yard in the middle of the party. He didn't care whose party it was. His girl was there along with his stepson and G Baby as he called Escolan.

"There's mommy!" Sky exclaimed excitedly.

The entire party looked up at the helicopter that was creating a massive noise. When Cash and Kellz locked eyes, her heart dropped and she froze. She wanted so bad to run, but he had already seen her. She slightly shook her head, and Breelah walked over to her and nudged her.

When the copter came to a complete stop, Skylar was the first to jump off.

"Mommy!" She ran into Cash's arms and hugged her as if she hadn't seen her in years.

Nino looked on confused because Cash hadn't once mentioned a child. From the side of her eyes, Cash could feel Nino watching her. She looked over in his direction, then turned to look at Kellz who was now walking up.

"Kellz!" Nino contentedly shouted.

"Nino?" Kellz spoke more of a questioned. He couldn't believe his eyes. As they hugged, he looked at Cash, and they held each other's gaze. Kellz's eyes were bloodshot red while Cash's eyes held a gloss.

After they embraced, Nino bent down to one knee in front of Sky. "What's your name, pretty girl?" he asked, and Skylar smiled.

"I'm Skylar. What's your name?"

"I'm Brooklyn, Skylar."

"Brooklyn like my brother." Sky giggled. "His dad's name is Brooklyn too, but he's in Heaven." Skylar's voice softened.

Nino looked back at Cash, and instead of being upset, he hit her with a faint smile. For some strange reason, he noticed how everyone was so timid, and he figured it was because Cash had a child. However, what Nino didn't know was, the entire mood shifted because Cash was now in a relationship with his best friend.

Cash waited for Kellz to drop the bomb on Nino, but to her surprise, he hadn't said a word. Every now and then he would look over and the pain in his eyes was evident. He was happy to see his best friend still alive, but right now he looked like a fool. Everyone knew this entire time but him. *So this where she been creeping off too,* Kellz thought to himself.

"Kellz, you want a bite to eat? Lil' Mama hook Kellz and Skylar up some food." Nino looked over.

"Okay." Cash spoke above a whisper and walked off to the food table.

The entire time, Kellz watched her pile food onto their plates. When she walked back over, she handed Kellz his plate and told Sky to come have a seat. She tried hard not to make eye contact with Kellz, but she couldn't help it. She apologetically looked him in the eyes but sorry wasn't good enough.

"Let's get back to partying," Nino spoke and grabbed Cash around the neck. He placed a kiss on her lips and Cash tried hard to pull back.

She was not only nervous of Kellz, who was watching everything, but she also was perturbed because she didn't want Skylar's big mouth to yell out that Kellz and Cash were together. Cash knew eventually she would have to tell Nino, and after what had just transpired, she was gonna have to talk to him tonight. Or at least she wanted to. It was Nino's birthday. How could she leave with Kellz?

"Nino, would you like to see my bomb?!" Skylar yelled

over to Nino as she bit into her steak.

"A bomb?" Nino looked around the table and everyone laughed.

It actually broke the ice, and now the attention was on Skylar. Sky pulled out her iPhone 11 and went to the pictures of her bomb that she had built. Everyone laughed thinking she was joking, but in fact, she had a picture of a bomb in her cell. Because of the decorations in the background, everyone knew it was her bedroom.

"Does it really blow up?" Nino asked, looking at Skylar awkwardly.

"Yes, silly." She giggled. "If you pull this plug, you have exactly 10 seconds to get out of the way." Again, she cracked herself up at how strangely everyone was acting. They acted like they hadn't seen a bomb, and it tickled Skylar. Skylar looked over to Jackie on the sly. Their eyes connected, but Jackie quickly turned her head.

"Skylar, why do you have a bomb, baby?" Cash asked curiously but worried.

"It's to protect you, Mommy. If the bad guys come to get you, I'm gonna blow they ass away."

"Skylar! Watch your mouth." Papi looked over to his baby sister.

"My bad." She covered her mouth, then looked back to her Mommy. "I always see how sad Liy Liy is without her mommy, so I don't ever want to be sad. I love you, Cash." Sky said seriously, and everyone around laughed.

It was a heartfelt moment, but she called her mother by her name, which told everyone she was serious. The child was treacherous already but had the most innocent look; just like Cash. However, Cash had created her own bomb that would more than likely blow up in her face.

While everyone was so in tune with one another, no one noticed Doctor Stine, who stood nearby observing everything that was taking place. His adrenaline was pumping, and he was eager to sit down and write. Cash's story was getting better and better, and it made him consider the spin off after all. He had already sat down with his mystery character, so he had some great content. Next week was his book event to release part two, and he couldn't wait until it was time to release part three. The first book went along with the movie, and after the explosion, no one expected a sequel. Doctor Stine was gonna take the world by surprise.

Cash didn't know about the book that had already been released, and Nino, who lived in his home for years, had no clue, either. They would soon find out but because Cash gave him written and verbal permission there was nothing anyone could do. Doctor Stine knew he was gonna rake up millions, and by the time he was done with parts two and three, then shot the movies to follow, he would be a billionaire enjoying the fruits of his hard labor.

CHAPTER 24

CASH LOPEZ

"Every time that I let you in
You take away something deep within
A fool for love is a fool for pain
But I refuse to love you again..."
-Lisa Fischer

One Week Later...

O ver the course of one week, Cash was happy to finally have Nino back home, but she was gloomy because of the way things went down with Kellz. The day after Nino's birthday gathering, Cash went home, and all Kellz's belongings were gone. When she noticed the ring she had copped him sitting on the dresser, her heart shattered even more. The ring was very sentimental to her, and he promised no matter what, he'd never remove it. He would always say he'd die with the ring on his finger, but that turned out to be a lie. She had called, texted and even sent an email, but received not one response or answer. Cash knew she killed him inside, and he deserved closure.

She wanted him to understand everything happened so fast. Nothing was intended, and she damn sure would never purposely hurt him. Yet he had to understand this was Brooklyn Nino. The only man she ever gave her heart to. Not only did they have a son, but they had history, they were married twice and they had caught numerous bodies together. Nino took the life of his own child's mother for her love. Nino wasn't just some ex. He was the man that Cash traded in the world for. Nino transformed her entire lifestyle. She had money, she was a savage at heart, accepted all, and added to her humanity.

"Where you going, Lil' Mama?" Nino asked, looking over Cash's attire.

"I have to make a run. Can you be ready by the time I get back?"

"Where we going?"

"Doctor Stine's book release signing."

"I thought you ain't wanna fuck with that shit?"

"Well, I changed my mind. I just wanna support him."

"A'ight. How long you gon' be gone?"

"About an hour. Two max."

"A'ight. Gimmie kiss." Nino smirked and pursed his lips.

He was in good spirits because he was back home in his castle where he belonged. It felt good to have his wife by his side. It felt even better to walk down a hall and everyone would light up. Unlike Doctor Stine's home where everything was so gloomy. His G Baby was getting used to him, and even Sky called his name every five minutes. And let him not forget Liyah. She was the daughter he never had. She was polite and well mannered. Liyah was always excited to be around Nino. Just like Cash, she felt secure. She felt bad for Kellz, but the King was home. Everything about Papi was different, and she was enjoying his vibes. He stayed home more, and she knew it was because of his father. Things were perfect in the Lopez residence with no scars.

Cash reached down to place a kiss on his lips, then left quickly because it was paining her to face him. She was happy Nino was home, but the truth still remained: Kellz was somewhere hurting. On the way out, Cash tried to move quickly through the home because she was avoiding everyone. However, Papi caught her dang bang.

"You need me to roll with you?" he asked, looking into her eyes.

"I'm good, son." Cash sighed and smiled at her son.

It always tripped her out how in tune he was with her. If she hurt, he hurt. And if it was time for war, he'd beat her to the punch. Nothing went over Papi's head because he was not only emotionally connected to his mother, but they were soul tied to one another. Like now. It was like their souls communicated without words. Papi knew exactly where his mother was going, and he commended her because she couldn't leave Kellz hanging. He was ecstatic his pops was back, but he wanted her to close that wound to a broken Kellz.

Cash walked out of the door and headed for the car. The driver already awaited her, so he stood by with the door opened. She climbed into the car, and they pulled out of the yard. The entire way, Cash rehearsed what she would say nervously. She was so deep in her thoughts she hadn't noticed they'd arrived. She apprehensively climbed out and made her way to the door. She knocked three times, and suddenly the door opened slowly. Cash stood face to face with Adrina, who had her arms folded across her chest. The moment she saw who stood at her door, her attitude skyrocketed.

"Cash," she spoke not pleased to see her.

"Where's Kelly?" Cash tried hard to hold her composure. For a brief moment, Drina didn't say a word. She only looked at Cash because she had her nerves showing up to her doorstep. Instead of Drina giving her a piece of her mind she called out to Kellz.

When Kellz appeared in the doorway, he was shocked to see Cash. He closed the door behind himself and Drina became furious. Kellz had told Drina exactly what transpired, so this eased Drina's curiosity about Kellz going back. However, she wanted Cash to know he was back home. Drina knew Kellz didn't stand a chance against Nino, so she didn't trip. She headed back into the kitchen and continued picking the greens for tonight's dinner.

"What's up, Cash?" Kellz asked without looking at her.

Cash took a moment to speak, and when she finally swallowed the lump in her throat, she turned to face him. "I'm sorry," she slightly whispered as tears began to form in her eyes.

"Nah, Lil' Mama. Them tears ain't gon' work," Kellz spoke sarcastically.

"I understand you're upset, but Kellz I swear I ain't mean for this to happen. I went to look for the Doctor, and when I showed up to his home with my loaded gun, Nino appeared from nowhere."

"But you could have told me, Cash." He spoke with force.

"How could I? Like, be for real. *Oh, hey, Kelly. By the way, my husband's really not dead.*" Cash shook her head with a *be for real* gesture. "I just couldn't, Kellz. I love you; I swear I do, but this is Brooklyn Carter we're talking about."

"There's nothing you can say to make me understand this situation. I been the nigga here holding you down. That's my boy, but, Cash, you was supposed to step up. It's good. You love him more." Kellz's voice cracked, and for the first time, Cash saw tears in his eyes. "Look, I understand. I can't even compete with Nino. You know how many times I've caught you staring at his picture crying? Cash, you will never love a man like you love him; even dead. Real shit, I love you, but I gotta pass the crown. You got your fairytale you always talked about." Tears finally escaped Kellz's face freely. He had no choice but to accept the truth.

"I don't want it to end like this."

"So what the fuck you want?" Kellz looked at her for an answer he knew he would get. "You gotta be kidding me?" Kellz grabbed his head. "You want to be with both of us?!" Kellz shrieked. When Cash remained quiet, he continued to chuckle. "Man, you gotta be fucking kidding. I'm not that nigga, Cash. I'll never be no side nigga to a bitch I love." Kellz was serious. He had never disrespected Cash, but right now he didn't care.

"But I guess it was cool I was a side bitch?" Cash now had a straight face.

"Fuck you talking about?"

"You fucking your ex-wife. Nigga, I saw the messages between y'all. You know why I ain't bust you across the head with my pistol? Because I knew I was the cause. Nigga, you didn't even know Nino was alive when you started sticking your dick back in her. But I sucked it up because I know I pushed you back into her arms. You ain't want Drina, and Drina far from a threat."

"See, that's where you wrong. I stuck my dick in her because I knew somebody was sticking theirs in you; I just didn't know it was Nino."

They both got quiet.

"How did you know I was there?" Cash asked a question she had been wondering all week.

"Don't matter," Kellz replied, embarrassed.

"You tracked my phone." Cash shook her head already knowing the answer.

Kellz didn't reply because he was caught. "So are you gonna tell him? I mean, he's gonna find out eventually. Don't lie to him the way you lied to me."

"I didn't lie to you."

"Cash, you been lying to me our whole damn relationship. And to answer your question, I ain't telling him shit. That's your job. Now run along. My wife and kids waiting on me." Kellz dismissed Cash as if she was nothing.

However, he was trying to run from reality. He couldn't stand to look at her because love didn't die overnight. He knew for the rest of his life Cash would hold a special place in his heart, but he had to let her go. When he looked at her, it pained him to see the many tears falling down her face. She looked at him for the last time with hurt in her eyes, and that told him she half-ass cared. He had just crushed her with his last words no matter the situation. Without another word, Cash walked away.

"Cash." Kellz spoke her name as if he knew this would be their last encounter. Cash turned to look at him, and even with the distance between them, she could see the tears falling from his eyes. "I'll always love you," Kellz poured out melancholy.

Cash didn't reply, but his words traveled through her body like an electric shock. She felt his words in not only her heart but her soul. She wouldn't admit it to him, but she felt the same way. Although Nino was the man of her dreams, she would always hold a special place in her heart for Kellz. She, too, knew this was the end, but she was gonna travel down that dark tunnel because at the end of it, Nino awaited her.

CHAPTER 25

DOCTOR STINE

"The best things in life are free
But you can keep them for the birds and bees
Now give me money
(That's what I want)..."
-The Beatles

Doctor Stine stood near the oversized banner that read Life After Love 2. He looked amongst his guests and was proud of his turn out. There were nearly five hundred people in attendance, so he would make a killing just in paperback sales. $50 a pop was his price with a signature. He was happy he purchased the signature stamp because he knew his fingers would go limp, but if need be, he would sign every book with a motive.

"Doctor, can we get a picture?" a lady walked over and wrapped her arms around Doctor Stine.

Charlotte stood off to the side in a jealous rage because every woman in the building was drooling over her husband. He wasn't dressed in his usual scrubs. Today he wore a three-piece suit and had gotten a fresh hairdo. Charlotte wondered if he worked with all the women, and because of today, she now hated his job. She was glad he had retired to become a full-time writer and filmmaker. She knew with fame came more women, so she decided to go to every event he hosted after today.

After several pictures, Doctor Stine walked over to his wife. Just as he was gonna speak, he noticed Cash and Nino walk through the door. He really didn't expect to see them because Cash mentioned she wouldn't be attending. Doctor Stine watched as the two showcased through the door, and it's like he fell into a trance. He was obsessed like a psychopath in a horror movie. He knew sooner or later his story would have to come to an end, so for weeks he wrecked his brain on the perfect ending. Just watching Cash and Nino now, he began to get crazy thoughts that consumed his mind insanely. They dominated the room, and he became envious in a financial way.

"Honey, stop drooling. His wife is with him." Doctor Stine nudged Charlotte.

"Drooling? I'm not droo—"

"Oh, you've drooled all over that man," Doctor Stine said sarcastically and laughed. "'*Oh my God Abdullah, it's sooo big,*'" he mimicked what he had heard on his tape. He was good and drunk, and today he would speak what was on his mind.

Charlotte looked at him strangely, and the way he looked told her exactly what he meant; he knew.

"Hey, Nino. Hey, Cash." Doctor Stine greeted them then escorted them over to an empty table. He quickly took Cash away from Charlotte because he didn't need the catty bickering at his event.

"You outdid yourself with this one." Cash looked around at the many people and the event's decor.

"Thank you." Doctor Stine smiled. What he wanted to say was, *on your expense,* but he kept the thought to himself. Doctor Stine excused himself from the table and went to make a call. He made sure he went to a quiet area in the event. For this call, he needed privacy because this was a moment he contemplated daily.

"Hey, David."

"Hey. Sorry to bother you. I'm gonna make this quick because I'm at my event."

"You had an event? Why didn't I get the invite? I'm sure I

could've snagged me a cute rich doctor."

"Oh, noooo," Doctor Stine replied, looking in the direction of Cash and Nino's table. "Hey, look. I have a really good ending. It's kinda crazy, but I think we'll go out with a bang. That way we could introduce your story. I'll call you tonight and run it by you."

"Okay."

"Hey," Doctor Stine called out on the edge.

"Yes?"

"I have to trust you on this one. You can never tell a soul."

"My word is my bond, Doctor Stine. You're messing with a real street bitch. Not some fiction character." The caller laughed.

"Atta girl." Doctor Stine smiled as he watched Nino stand from his seat. Nino walked over to the bar, and moments later, Charlotte headed in the same direction. Doctor Stine shook his head at how bold Charlotte had become. It was bad enough she was screwing the man in their home, but at his event was just a bit over the edge.

Charlotte walked over to Nino as he waited for the bartender to hand him the bottle of Champagne he ordered. He didn't see Charlotte, but the smell of her cheap perfume in a distance told him she was near.

"Abdullah, he knows."

Nino turned around to the sound her voice. "What you mean, he knows?"

"He knows. I don't know. I think he has a camera or some sort of recorder in the house." Charlotte spoke nervously because of the comment he had made.

"Damn." Nino looked at her to see if she was serious. He then turned around to find Doctor Stine, and his heart dropped. He was seated at the table next to Cash. When he noticed Nino watching him, he lifted his glass and hit him with a head nod. He stood to his feet then whispered something into Cash's ear. "Whatever it is, you better fix this shit. If that nigga tell my wife anything about us, you and him both dead. Oh, and you'll meet

Nino; not Abdullah," Nino threatened then walked away.

He was serious. For Cash, he would kill just as he had done before. He killed his son's mother because she had caused chaos between him and Cash. Therefore, Charlotte needed to figure this shit out before she met her maker. Due to the stories she'd heard about Nino, she knew he was serious. She had to think and think quickly.

***

After a long day, Doctor Stine was good and drunk off the many flukes of champagne he had guzzled. All the way home, he had Charlotte drowning in sorrow by his disgusting choice of words. He called her every name in the book except for a child of God. Over a dozen times, he reminded her that when they got home, she needed to pack her things and leave. Charlotte was distraught because she had nowhere to go while Nino was probably sleeping peacefully with his wife. Although she had deceived her husband, he was acting like an egotistical maniac. Charlotte knew it was more than just her sleeping with Nino because long ago he had fallen out of love. Now that he had the deal of a lifetime, Charlotte was no use to him, and she read between the lines.

When they walked into the house, Charlotte headed up the hall for their bedroom to begin packing. There was no reasoning with him, so she chose to remain quiet. Tears poured from her eyes as she began tossing items into an oversized suitcase. Once she was done, she threw a few items into a huge Nike tote and the rest would have to stay. She draped the tote across her chest and locked her fingers into the belt of the suitcase. She made her way down the hall but stopped when she heard her husband's voice. The sound of the woman's voice blurred throughout the room, and the way she greeted David made Charlotte sick to her stomach. Not being able to contain herself, Charlotte left her suitcase in the hall and opened the door.

"Why aren't you gone?" Doctor Stine asked, irritated with

her presence.

"I don't have anywhere to go." Charlotte was hoping her tears would make him change his mind.

"Well, that's not my problem. Now get the hell out." Doctor waved his hand to dismiss her.

Charlotte dropped her head and headed for the door with nothing left to say. Just as she was making her way out, she noticed the small recording device along with a small head set. The device piqued Charlotte's interest, and something told her this was the device that David used to discover the affair with her and Nino. Charlotte looked back, and when she noticed David wasn't paying attention, she scooped the headset up and slyly hit record on the device. Charlotte left the room curiously and walked out of the home. When she made it to her vehicle, she tossed it in her belongings, then climbed behind the wheel.

She looked at the small headset and slid it inside of her ear. She was eager to find out if David was cheating on her, but what she didn't know was, she would stumble upon something much more interesting. She listened to David and the mysterious woman's phone call, and she began to place the pieces together. They discussed a book. Not just any book, but a book that would damage Nino and Cash. She was gonna use this information to make a few bucks, then she would disappear forever.

CHAPTER 26

BROOKLYN NINO

*"It's safe to say I earned it, ain't a nigga gave me nothin'
I'm ready to hop out on a nigga, get to bustin'
Know you heard me say, "You play, you
lay, " don't make me push the button
Full of pain, dropped enough tears to fill up a fuckin' bucket..."*
-Da Baby

Nino laid back on the bed he now shared with Cash Lopez breezing through the pages of Doctor Stine's book. After what Charlotte had told him at the event, it made him wonder what was on the inside of those pages. The first book was about the explosion, and there was nothing to leave him wondering about. Therefore, he moved to the second part and began reading from the first page. It had been hours since he'd been trying to decipher the story because somethings just wasn't adding up. He hadn't made it to the part about he and Charlotte, but something more interesting caught his attention. He mentioned Bernice, who was Cash's character, engaged in an affair with Abdullah's best friend. As Nino continued to read, it all began to make perfectly good sense.

Kellz was the only one of his friends still alive, so he had to be the best friend he mentioned. Doctor Stine referred to Kellz as Michael, but it didn't take a scientist to figure it out. The more Nino read, the more he became angry. The novel was fully detailed, even telling about Cash having Skylar by some doctor. When he'd gotten near the end, he read something about a movie theater. Nino pulled out his phone and began searching movie theaters nearby. After scrolling through several theaters, he stopped when he noticed the name *Brooklyn Cinema*. He clicked on the page and began browsing the many photos. Finally, he reached a photo of the owners and the headline read *Miami Couple Opens Urban Theater*. It was a picture of Kellz and Cash holding hands. He then scrolled to an entirely different picture, and there it was: a picture of Kellz and Cash kissing right there in front of the establishment.

Nino slammed the book closed and jumped to his feet. He began pacing the floor trying hard to contain his anger. He tried to reason with himself about the affair, but he couldn't justify Cash's action. He understood he had been gone for a long time and things happened, but the fact that both of them failed to mention they were a couple was snake shit in his eyes. He thought back to the day of his event and began shaking his head. Everyone was acting weird, and for some reason, Cash looked nervous. *That's why that nigga had Skylar*, Nino thought as he continued to pace. Finally reaching his boiling point, Nino grabbed his newly purchased phone and a set of keys to one of Cash's cars. He flew out the door and headed for Papi's bedroom. When he walked in, Papi was laid back with his son asleep on his chest, and Liyah sat at the foot of the bed writing in a notebook.

"Let me holla at you, BJ." Nino tried hard to keep a straight face.

Papi could sense something wasn't right and knew exactly what it could be. He lifted from the bed and laid the baby down on his stomach. He headed out the room, and Nino was right behind him.

"So you knew about it?"

"About what, Pops?"

"About yo' moms fucking Kellz."

Again, Papi began shaking his head because he knew eventually this would happen. He told his mother over and over to tell Nino what was going on, and each time she said she needed time. Now that the time had come, Papi was stuck between a rock and hard place.

"Yeah, I knew. But, Dad, that was up to yo' wife to tell you. You my pops, and that's my mother. You gotta understand that lady has been the one here with me, so I owe her some sort of loyalty. Please don't put me in this shit because all y'all grown." Papi stood up to his father.

Nino loved his reply, and this was, indeed, his son. However, he couldn't glorify Papi right now because he had big fish to fry.

"I respect that." Nino nodded and watched his son briefly. Nino broke the eye contact by heading down the stairs.

"Aye, Nino!" Papi called out to him. "Don't do no crazy shit. A nigga need you out here," Papi spoke sincerely.

The words Papi had spoken made Nino feel every bit of it, and he was right. Nino had to think wisely because he couldn't risk missing out on the rest of Papi's life. It already pained him that he'd been absent for nearly two decades, so he couldn't move loosely.

When Nino made it outside, he hit the alarm and Cash's Aston Martin's light flickered. He strolled coolly to the car and climbed in. He didn't bother turning on the music because he needed to collect his thoughts. He pulled out of the driveway and headed for the highway. He had been gone for so long he wasn't sure if Kellz lived in the same home that he and Drina once shared, but he was gonna chance it. He pushed the pedal to the metal and was there in record time. Just his luck Drina was in the front yard as if her and the children just pulled in. Nino swooped the car into the driveway and climbed out.

"Nino." Drina smiled, happy to see him. He gave her a warming hug and they began to make small talk. After a few minutes, Nino didn't wanna be rude, but he was on a mission.

"Is Kellz here?"

Drina paused briefly, then looked at Nino. "They're at the laundromat."

"Laundromat?" Nino asked, confused.

"Yes. Kelly owns a chain of laundromats. Says he needed to collect his money and sign some papers." Drina shrugged as if she knew nothing.

Nino read between the lines, and he also caught that statement about *they're at the laundromat,* in reference to the two of them. After Drina gave him the address, he hugged her once more then climbed back into the car. He punched the address into his navigation, then headed for the location.

***

"Kellz, I keep telling you I'm not about to take your laundromat."

"Look, Cash, I understand I copped them with my bread, but you the one helped me run 'em, so it's only right."

"But we're not married, so I'm not taking them."

Nino stood by the door listening to Cash and Kellz bicker back and forth about the businesses. Ready to get it over with, he stepped into the office, and they both looked up astounded. Nino took a seat at the table and the room fell silent. He waited for someone to speak, and when he noticed the cat had their tongues, he decided to initiate the conversation.

"What's up with you two love birds?"

"Look, Brook, it's not what—"

"What I think? I know you ain't 'bout to pull that one, Cash. It's exactly what I think. Now the problem here is, why the fuck I'm the last one to find out?" Nino looked in between the two of them.

"I was gonna tell you, Nino," Cash replied truthfully.

"When?!" Nino jumped to his feet and flung the chair across the room.

"Man, look, Nino. I apologize for what went on between Cash and I, but it's over between us. I'm just trying to be a stand up nigga and give her a few of these establishments."

"She doesn't need your establishments. Daddy back

home. She don't need shit from no nigga," Nino shot, and Kellz threw his hands up. "This shit is embarrassing. Y'all whole love affair is inside of that man's book. From the day you had Skylar until the day Que was killed."

Cash replayed Nino's words, and she stopped to listen further. Nino continued to talk about the book, and it never dawned on Cash that all along Doctor Stine knew she was alive. This entire time he had been watching Cash and Kellz. *He knew I was alive,* Cash thought to herself, and this information pulled her train of thoughts from what Nino was saying.

"Nigga, you the one told me fuck with her. You the one said to marry her if I had to so I could protect her," Kellz voiced with irritation.

Again, Cash stopped to look at both men. "Is this true?' Cash asked somberly.

Nino didn't respond, and the look Kellz now wore told her that it was, in fact, true.

"Cash, I did it to protect you," Kellz replied, seeing how hurt she looked.

"Well, some type of protection because this entire time this fucking doctor has been watching me. All along he knew I was alive, and all along he kept Nino locked away from us for a damn story." Tears began to fall from Cash's eyes, and she turned to run away.

"Cash!" Nino tried to stop her, but she didn't bother to turn around. He thought of what she said about Doctor Stine, and it never dawned on him. How could he possibly know about Kellz and Cash's relationship? He knew about the movie theater and all, and this told him he knew Cash was alive all along.

"Oh, some rich white man bought the Lopez estate. I went by to see if I could shoot some scenes."

Nino thought back to the day Doctor Stine lied. The more he thought about it, the angrier he became. The situation with Kellz had to wait because he had someone he needed to kill.

"Nino," Kellz called out to him. He tossed him a cell phone and Nino looked at it puzzled. "Tracker." Kellz raised an

154

eyebrow and Nino caught on to exactly what he meant.

Nino flew out of the establishment and raced home in search of Cash. He already had plans to kill Doctor Stine before he told Cash about Charlotte, and now the doctor gave him even more reason to end his life. This would be Nino's first kill after nearly twenty years, and it hungered him. He was ready to take Doctor Stine's life with no mercy, although the doctor caused lots of mercy on him.

CHAPTER 27

KANGO & PAPI AALIYAH
& ENFINITY

"Baby you gotta know that I'm just out here doing
What I gotta do for me and you and we eating
So bitch, why the fuck is you tripping?
I'm taking these chances..."
-Lil Wayne

Spreading her ass cheeks open, Kango slid every inch into Fin's wet pussy. The sound of ass clapping filled the air along with the smell of peach body wash and sex. Sweat poured down Kango's forehead, but he continued to blow Fin's back out. Every so often, she would try to get away from him, and he would pull her back and pound harder. Right now, the two were going through what Kango called some bullshit, all because Mahogany had called his phone. Kango promised Fin he hadn't talked to Mahogany since the day they had left the club together.

Although it was a lie, Kango had really dismissed her to repair his relationship with Fin. After everything that had been happening around him, we wanted to walk a straight narrow line with no distractions. He watched how Jackie's love story unfolded, and now he was a witness to the destruction going on with Cash and Nino. Kango didn't want his love story to pan out with hate and harboring ill feelings. He wanted to live happy and be a father soon.

"Kanon, baby, I'm about...Ughhhhhhh!"

Fin couldn't complete her sentence because she was in the process of releasing one of the world's greatest nuts. Her body was shaking, her pussy was dripping and Kanon fucked her as if he had something to prove.

Just as he began to plunge into her again, her phone rang. When she heard the "That's My Dawg" ringtone, she asked Kango to give her a min. Kango looked at her in disbelief because no matter what they were in the middle of, she would stop the world to attend to Aaliyah. He understood the love they shared for one another, but, nah. Something just wasn't right. He was dicking her down with the best dick she ever had, and here she was ready to pull off and run out on him.

Fin could hear the sigh from Kango as he pulled out of her. Pussy sore and legs on fire, Fin still wobbled over to grab her phone. When she answered, Liyah spoke in code. After replying, Fin looked at Kango apprehensively. She knew he was gonna be upset, but she couldn't help his feelings. He knew the deal when it came to the hustle. He just didn't know his girl was hustling. With the kind of money they were racking up, Fin had become obsessed with hustling. She would drop anything she was doing to chase her bag. Therefore, she would have to take a rain check and catch Kango later when she made it back home.

"I be back, bae." Fin slid into her clothing without looking in his direction. She then headed into the restroom to wash up.

Kango continued to shake his head as he dressed and prepared to leave. He didn't bother saying another word to Fin. He headed out of the door and into the den to wrap with Ace. He needed to have a man on man talk, and after learning about Ace's past, he knew he was the best candidate for the conversation.

Back upstairs, Fin quickly dressed then made her way out of the door. When she made it downstairs, Jackie was seated on the sofa eating ice cream and watching *Maury*. She and Fin looked at each other, and Fin smiled to assure her exactly where she was going.

"Be safe," Jackie called out to her.

"Always." Fin winked and walked out to her car.

"Sup, sis? Kango in there?" Papi asked as he stepped outta of his black on black Bentley coupe.

"Yeah, he's in there. I think he's in the den."

"A'ight."

Papi jogged up to the door, and Fin made her way out the gate. She jumped on the highway to meet Liyah at the warehouse. Brandon had called and said they were all out of product, so the girls needed to make the trip down to Cuba to cop.

Back inside the home, Jackie's mind began to flutter with thoughts, and she had a weird feeling in the pit of her stomach. All through the night she had mild contractions, but this feeling didn't come from the baby. It was one of those eerie feelings like something tragic was gonna take place. Jackie sat the tub of ice cream down and picked up her phone. She needed to check some traps, but not just any traps.

"Espinoza."

"Hey, it's Jackie."

"Oh, hey, Jack. I was just gonna call you. Hold on a sec. Let me grab these documents. I have some interesting news for you." Espinoza sat the phone down briefly and was back within seconds. "Okay, let's see what we have. Allen Joseph checked out with not even a ticket. Kevin Conland has some petty theft from 2008. Now this Timothy kid is just a menace. Meth head, GTA several times and he was arrested for a firearm. Did six months and was released because he was a minor. Now hold on to the fly of your seat. Brandon Hebrew. Good kid, but his father is head of the ATF," Espinoza continued, but everything after was a blur.

"ATF?!" Jackie jumped to her feet appalled. "If there was any foul play with his father, wouldn't you know?"

"Not necessarily. If it's out of our jurisdiction, then, no. Now if you paid for that jurisdiction, then, yes."

"Of course, it's about the money. Well, thank you. I'll call you later." Jackie ended the call nervously.

"Jack, you good?" Kango asked sensing something was wrong.

"No." Jackie looked at Kango and Papi, who had just emerged from upstairs. "Please don't be upset. It's about Fin and Liyah. I think they're in trouble—Ouhhhh!" Jackie grabbed her stomach and doubled over.

"You good?" Papi grabbed her.

"I don't know. I think I'm going into labor." Jackie's face scrunched. She began breathing in and out, but she needed to tell the fellas what was going on. "Kango, call my father," she managed to squeeze in between her breathing. "Look, you guys need to go down to the old warehouse on Beach behind the factories. Fin and Liyah are there and the police could possibly be watching. Here, take this." Jackie handed Papi a gadget with a small pin.

"Wait, why would the police be watching Fin and Liyah? And what the fuck they doing in a warehouse?" Papi asked, because Liyah and Fin were supposed to be at the mall. Or at least that's what Liyah told Papi.

"You'll see when you get there."

"What's this?"

"There's a bomb inside of the warehouse. If you need to use it, pull that pin out and push that button," Jackie instructed. Both men looked at her as if she was crazy. Like, who the hell walked around with a bomb clipped on their keys? "I know, I know, who walks around with a bomb? Well, look. Those girls are into some heavy shit, so I just had to be prepared. And you can thank your little sister for that." Jackie nodded, referring to Skylar. "Let's just pray it works." She walked off holding her back. By the time she made it to the stairs, a gush of water came raining down her legs.

"Oh, my. My water just broke."

***

After making sure Jackie was off to the hospital, the fellas jumped into the unmarked car Jackie kept with no plates. They headed to the warehouse Jackie had given them the directions to. When they arrived, nothing looked out of place except Liyah's pink Bugatti that sat out front. Papi shook his head because whatever they were into, they were dumb as hell to have had that car out front. On cue, they both climbed out and made their way inside. When Papi opened the door, he stepped inside and couldn't believe his eyes.

"You see this shit?" Papi turned to Kango.

"Yeah, I see it, but look at this shit?" Kango pointed to Liyah and Fin who sat over by the table sorting out the Meth. "Get y'all dumb asses over here!" Papi's voice echoed around the warehouse.

Both Liyah and Fin quickly turned around. They were startled by the sound of Papi's voice, and when they realized they were caught, they became nervous.

"Oh, shit, 5-0 is coming!" Kev shouted from the door.

"Let's go!" Kango told the girls, and they dropped everything they were doing to make a dash for it. The sound of police sirens were getting near, and both girls began to panic. They followed Papi out of the back door and climbed into the car they had come in. They quickly pulled off, and just as they made it a few feet away, Papi stopped the car.

"Papi, what are you doing?!" Liyah asked worriedly. "Why aren't you driving?!"

"Liyah, shut the fuck up!" Papi watched as the swarm of police ran into the warehouse.

"Is that Brandon?" Fin pointed to Brandon who was in the back of a squad car. The girls looked at one another, and something wasn't right.

"I hope this works." Papi pulled the pin from his pocket. He did as Jackie told him: he pulled the pin out then hit the button. He remembered hearing Sky say ten seconds, so he counted five seconds in his head, then pushed the pedal to the metal.

BOOM!

The sound of the explosion could be heard in the distance. Papi and Kango looked at one another in disbelief. The explosion was so powerful, Papi was sure everyone back there was dead. Liyah must have been thinking the same thing because she uttered the words *Timothy,* and her heart broke into a million pieces. She remained quiet, and it was as if Fin could read her mind. Their eyes communicated with one another, and a flush of sadness flushed through their bodies. They had grown to love Timothy, and his memory would forever live through them. Fin grabbed Liyah's hand tightly, and neither of them spoke a word. They silently prayed for their friend. They were so hurt and defeated they could care less about being chewed out by their men. Timothy meant a lot to them, and because of them, he was dead.

CHAPTER 28

BROOKLYN NINO & CASH LOPEZ

"Love like ours is Heaven-sent
Each day a day to remember
I feel so safe, feel secure with you."
-Anita Baker

Nino called Cash's phone over a dozen times and got no answer. Right now he was still upset by the way her and Kellz played things out, but it wasn't the time. He knew Cash like a book. Therefore, he knew she was out causing destruction. He sent her a text that Jackie had gone into labor, and even that didn't work. He began pacing the floor—something he did when something was heavy on his mind. He had to think of a way to talk her out of whatever she was about to do. Nino knew Cash had no problem getting her hands dirty, but he wanted her to leave that up to him. He wasn't no Kellz. Cash wasn't gonna be running around town bodying niggas while he set back twirling his thumbs.

Suddenly, the sound of commotion from downstairs made him stop to listen. When he heard Papi yelling, he flew out of the door to see what was going on. He ran down the stairs and realized it was Papi and Liyah arguing. Fin was sitting on the sofa, and Kango stood over by the kitchen upset.

"Y'all two dumb muthafuckas, yo'! Anything could have happened to y'all! If it wasn't for Jackie, y'all dumb muthafuckas would be sitting in a fucking cell right now!" Papi was enraged. His veins popped out the side of his neck as he spoke, and this told Liyah the level of anger he was battling with. She couldn't do anything but drop her head. Papi pulled out his phone and began dialing his mother. He put the phone on speaker, and when Cash answered, Nino looked over. Liyah became nervous because she knew Cash would be disappointed in her.

"Mama! Yo' fucking daughter and her damn side kick just almost went down!"

"What you mean went down?"

"These two asses have been lying about school this whole time. All along, they asses been at a damn warehouse that look like some shit out a movie." Papi looked at Liyah, then Fin, and shook his head. "Mama, I wish you could have seen that shit. These muthafuckas got a whole damn operation going on selling Meth."

"What?!" Cash's voice blared through the phone.

Liyah's heart dropped.

"How they get away?"

"Thanks to Jackie, she had a bomb inside just in case 5 came. These two idiots didn't even know. But trip this, Jackie got the bomb from yo' daughter; and it worked," Papi added, still shocked by his little sister's creativity. The sound of a helicopter could be heard in the background. It was so loud it began to drown out Cash's voice.

"I'll deal with their asses as soon as I get back. I gotta go," Cash spoke into the phone. Before she could hang up, Nino quickly took the phone from Papi's hand.

"Cash," he called her name, but there was too much noise in the background. "Cash!" he called out a second time, but the phone went dead. He handed Papi back his phone and ran upstairs to his bedroom. Just as he made it, his phone rang in his pocket. He quickly answered in hopes of it being Cash, but it was an unknown number.

"Hello?"

"Nino?" the caller spoke, and Nino knew exactly who the voice belonged to: Charlotte.

"Yeah."

"Nino, I need help, please. David threw me out of the house, and I have nothing or nowhere to go."

"What the fuck that gotta do with me?"

"What do you mean? All of this we created together."

"Look, Charlotte, we ain't create shit. That's yo' husband, so you work that shit out with him. Nigga knew all along because his bitch ass been snaking us the whole time."

"That's what I wanna talk to you about. I have some information for you. If you can give me a couple hundred grand, I can disappear after telling you this."

"I'm listening."

"David is planning on killing Cash. I overheard him talking to a woman, and whoever she is she knows Cash pretty well. Their planning to kill Cash for the ending of a book."

"The fuck?!" Nino shouted and grabbed his gun from the closet. He tucked it into his pants and headed out the door. He didn't know how much truth was behind Charlotte's story, but he couldn't take that chance. From the sound of the chopper in Cash's background, he knew she was on her way to Doctor Stine's. He just hoped he could make it in time to warn her.

***

Getting off the helicopter, Cash noticed Doctor Stine's car parked in his normal spot. As she walked over to the door, Kona began to bark distinctively. It was something about the growl Cash couldn't put her finger on, but she paid it no mind. She brushed her hand under Kona's neck just as she always did. Kona began rubbing her head against Cash's leg, and she continued to cry out. Cash made her way up the stairs and began knocking on the door roughly.

"Hey, Cash," Doctor Stine answered as if he was surprised to see her.

"I need to talk to you, David." Cash barged into the home. When she walked in, the house was dark, and there was an eerie feeling that lingered in the air. Cash being Cash, she pulled her pistol from her waist and pointed it to David.

"Woooah, woooah." Doctor Stine threw his hands up nervously. "Is everything okay?"

"You tell me."

"Cash, put the gun away. Let's talk about this."

"There's really nothing to talk about. This entire time you've been building a story around my life, and it was premeditated. You knew all along I was alive." Cash's finger snuggled tighter around the trigger. She was itching to end David's life, and there was no way he could talk himself out of it.

"I'm an author, Cash." David's face became more serious. He didn't have that same nervousness, and Cash could tell by his demeanor. "I couldn't let this opportunity pass me by. I made pretty good money off your story. Oh, and let's not forget your husband fucking my wife made a great storyline." David laughed sinisterly.

Cash looked at him puzzled, but she knew there was truth behind what David said because of the way Charlotte acted when she was around.

"So all this because my husband was fucking your wife?"

"Oh, no. All this for fame. I did something no doctor in the world could do. I'm the reason your husband is alive, and you owe me that."

"I don't owe nobody shit." Cash went to squeeze the trigger and before she could shoot...

Pop!

A single shot echoed throughout the home.

"Arhhhh!" Cash fell to the ground with a bullet pierced through her leg. She began firing off shots, but Doctor Stine had already dove out of the way. Suddenly, the light came on and another figure appeared into view.

"Kamela?" Cash spoke bemused.

"Cash Lopez," Kamela replied anxiously. She felt superior knowing she would be the one to take Cash's life.

David walked back over, and he took a seat on the chair. He hit record on his tape recorder and, this was the ending he had dreamed of.

"You know you're dead, right?" Cash spoke to Kamela without an ounce of fear. Kamela looked at her as if she had lost her mind because she had run out of bullets, and she was still tough. "Kamela, you're not a killer. Oh, Liyah is the killer out of you two. You're weak just like your mother." Cash laughed tauntingly.

"Fuck you, bitch. And fuck Aaliyah. After I kill you, your little Trap Princess is dead along with your son." Kamela spoke upon the ending of her spinoff story. "None of this had to come to this, but when y'all killed my father, shit got personal." Kamela went to pull the trigger to end Cash's life, but the door came crashing in, and Kona flew full speed and attacked Kamela. She began screaming gruesomely as Kona chewed at her legs.

"Kona!" Doctor Stine screamed for the dog, but Kona wouldn't let up. Doctor Stine rushed over to stop the attack, and Kamela called his name pensively.

"Doctor Stine!" Kamela called out, but it wasn't because of Kona.

"A red... a red..."

Pop!

Doctor Stine's head busted open like a pumpkin. Kamela screamed in fear never getting the chance to tell him about the infra-red dot on his forehead. Kamela called him repeatedly, but his head had been detached from his body.

"Damn, Kamela. Looks like y'all story went out with a bang." Cash laughed and now stood on one leg.

Kamela's legs were pouring blood from the many holes Kona had chewed in her. She began to cry dramatically in hopes Cash would spare her life. However, Kamela knew when it came to Cash, no one's life would be spared. It was always kill or be killed, and because she didn't get the chance to kill her, she knew she was dead.

"Kiss your father good bye, bitch." Cash pulled the trigger just as Nino and Papi walked through the door. Cash looked over to the two and let out a deep sigh. It seemed like they couldn't catch a break. Everyone in the world seemed to be against them, and she knew it was only a matter of time before someone else tried to get them.

"Damn. Kamela did have some good pussy." Papi stood over her dead body shaking his head.

"Papi!" Cash called out to him, and he shrugged his shoulders.

"Get me out of here so I can get stitched up. And after I'm done, I'm beating your ass, Nino." Cash hit him with a side-eye.

"What I do?"

"You fucked that man's wife."

"Ugh, you fucked that lady?" Papi scrunched his face, then fell into a fit of laughter.

"Shit, I ain't had no pussy for over ten years." Nino threw his hands up and everyone laughed. He swooped Cash into his arms, and before he carried her out, he whispered in her ear, "Her pussy wasn't as good as yours, Mrs. Carter."

Cash looked at him and couldn't help but laugh. "I love you forever, husband."

"Always."

THE END...

EPILOGUE

"I hereby give all proceeds and rights to Cash Carter. I'm sorry, but it's only right Mrs. Ingram. Those books and that movie was about her life. First, he did it without permission and then he used these people's lives to not only profit, but make a mockery out of. My decision is final."

Bang!

The judge banged his gavel, and Cash stood to her feet smiling. She turned to her family, and everyone was excited. Cash and Nino were now the owners of the movie *Halo* and every book that Doctor David Stine had ever written. All proceeds would be transferred into her account, which was well over 3 billion dollars. After thanking her attorney, Cash walked out of the courtroom with her head held high and her family right by her side. She had made the decision to pass the third book to Liyah so she could finish off the story. Cash had hired an editor and another author to help Liyah pan out the content. She was gonna continue Doctor Stine's legacy, but his family wouldn't get a dime.

When Cash stepped outside of the court building, there were tons of News reporters waiting for her. This was the biggest news in the tabloids, and it had created a story of its own. Cash looked at Jackie Snow, who had stepped out of the car with her son, and she hit Cash with a smirk.

Jackie had given birth to a baby boy she named Kango Ace. He weighed seven pounds and six ounces, and he was a split imagine of Capone. Already, Cash had fallen in love with little Kango and thought about giving her husband a child.

Kango and Papi were still heavy in the game and were now stepping up to run Jackie's empire. Liyah decided to collaborate on the book with Fin so they didn't have to hustle themselves. Fin's shop had now been transitioned into a lash bar with top-of-the-line doctors for permanent eyelash surgery. Liyah had found her location for her male exotic club she planned to open.

Like always, the Lopez family reigned on top, and everything in their lives were kosher. Love was blossoming for everyone because even Ace and Aunt Jean were showing suspicious acts of flirtation. Jackie was all for it and prayed one day love would fall to her feet.

As Cash Lopez made her way down the stairs of the courthouse, she was bombarded with questions from the many reporters. She tried hard to ignore them, but one question stood out and she stopped in her tracks.

"Mrs. Carter, how does it feel to have been reconnected with your husband after nearly two decades?"

"I'm standing in the light of his halo; I have my angel now," Cash replied honorably.

Nino grabbed her hand and led her down the rest of the stairs. He then escorted her into the vehicle, and before closing the door, she looked at her husband.

"I can feel your halo, Nino." She smiled and it warmed Nino's heart.

Back at Kellz's home, he sat on the sofa watching as Cash made her way out of the courthouse. The part that killed him was the statement Cash had finally made to the reporter. He noticed the change in Cash's face when she looked into the camera. It was like she could feel Kellz was watching, and there was meaning behind her statement. Although his heart had broken into a million pieces, Kellz was happy for Cash. He knew that for years she lived in misery, and no one could repair the hurt but Nino. He stood to his feet and walked into the kitchen to find Drina. He wrapped his arms around her and kissed into her neck.

"I love you," he told her, causing Drina to smile.

However, she knew better because she knew his heart was

with Cash. She knew Kellz loved her, but she also felt like she was just a rebound. She was gonna take it for what it was, and maybe one day, she could make him fall timeously in love with her, just as Cash had done.

Visit My Website
http://authorbarbiescott.com/?v=7516fd43adaa

Barbie Scott Book Trap
https://www.facebook.com/
groups/1624522544463985/
Like My Page On Facebook
https://www.facebook.com/
AuthorBarbieScott/?modal=composer
Instagram:
https://www.instagram.com/authorbarbiescott

Made in the USA
Middletown, DE
09 October 2020